SAINT DEATH

ALSO BY MARCUS SEDGWICK

Blood Red, Snow White

The Ghosts of Heaven

Midwinterblood

Revolver

She Is Not Invisible

White Crow

SAINT DEATH

MARCUS SEDGWICK

ROARING BROOK PRESS
NEW YORK

Copyright © 2016 by Marcus Sedgwick
Published by Roaring Brook Press
Roaring Brook Press is a division of Holtzbrinck Publishing Holdings Limited Partnership
175 Fifth Avenue, New York, New York 10010
fiercereads.com

First published in the United Kingdom in 2016 by Orion Children's Books, London

Cataloging-in-Publication Data is on file at the Library of Congress
ISBN 978-1-62672-549-2

Our books may be purchased in bulk for promotional, educational, or business use. Please contact
your local bookseller or the Macmillan Corporate and Premium Sales Department at
(800) 221-7945 ext. 5442 or by e-mail at MacmillanSpecialMarkets@macmillan.com.

First American edition 2017

Book design by Elizabeth H. Clark
Printed in the United States of America

1 3 5 7 9 10 8 6 4 2

For Ian Diment and Artur Santos
And for my father, who would have understood

This book is about other stories that occur over there,
across the river.
The comfortable way to deal with these stories is to say
they are about them.
The way to understand these stories is to say
they are about us.

—CHARLES BOWDEN (1945–2014)

THE RIVER

Not too far away from here, just over the horizon of our imagination, there's a girl floating in the river. She moves with the water, whispering through the bulrushes by the bank. Her arms are out to the side, her legs splay, and tiny fish dance around her toes. The hot sun warms her body against the cool of the water, which ripples peacefully as she drifts. A change in the current at the turn of the bend shifts her course and she floats out away from the bank, toward the center, uncaring, heedless.

Her only clothes are a stained tank top, and panties with Mickey Mouse on the front, a failed guardian angel. She picks up speed, and the far shore approaches, coming closer, until finally, a strong eddy takes her plump body and rolls her over, facedown in the water. She doesn't react.

There is little left to show who she was; her body says she was a young woman, but it's hard to judge her age; her head is wrapped in thick electrical tape, leaving only a thin slit for her nostrils. She lay at the bottom of the river for two days before the bloating brought her to the top, pushing her arms and legs away from her body.

When the police find her, *if* they find her, when they write a report, *if* they write a report, they'll say she drowned, just another mojado, another "wetback," and she drowned while trying to cross the river. Never mind the tape around her head. Never mind she was almost naked. Never mind the marks on her body.

Now, tantalizing, her fingers stroke the northern shore of the river. Over here, they call it Río Bravo. Over there, they call it Rio Grande, for that is El Norte: America.

ANAPRA

It doesn't look like the most dangerous place on earth. It looks like somewhere half-made, it looks like an aborted thought. It looks like a three-year-old god threw together some cardboard boxes and empty coffee tins and Coke bottles in the sandpit of the Chihuahuan desert, and then forgot it. Left it to its own vices. The god was forgetful and has not returned to care for his creation, but other gods, pitiless ones, are approaching even now, in a speeding pickup truck.

There's no more than a hurried moment to look around this careworn land. A dozen of the roads are paved: cracked concrete and full of holes; the rest are just rutted strips of dirt. Most of the houses aren't houses at all, but jacales: shacks made of packing crates and sheets of corrugated iron, of cardboard and of crap, with roofs of plastic sheeting or tar paper held down with old car tires. The best have cinder-block walls. The worst take more effort to imagine than is comfortable. Few have running water. One or two have stolen electricity using hookups from the power lines, a dangerous trick in a world made of sun-baked cardboard and wood.

The jacales are things that might, some distant day, be the ghostly ancestors of actual houses. When those houses are finally built, they will be built on lines of hope—the grid that's already been optimistically scratched far out into the desert in the belief that this place can become a thriving community. Already, there are attempts to make this a normal kind of place: whitewashed cinder-block houses with green tin roofs, the Pemex gas station, a primary school, a secondary school. There's even the new hospital, up the hill. The Del Rio store on the corner of Raya and Rancho Anapra, the main drag through the town. But these are exceptions, and all this, all of this, is founded on a belief that needs to ignore what is rapidly approaching in the truck.

This is the Colonia de Anapra, a little less than a shantytown, trying hard to be a little bit more than a slum; poorest of all the poor colonias of Juárez. And Juárez? Juárez is the beast, the fulminating feast of violence and of the vastly unequal wielding of power; where the only true currencies are drugs, guns, and violence. Juárez is a new monster in an old land: Juárez is the laboratory of our future.

Juárez, from where the pickup truck approaches at pace, lies down the hill. Anapra is just a small feeder fish, clinging to the belly of the whale, and while it doesn't look like the most dangerous place on earth, it is here as much as anywhere else where drugs are run and bodies are hanged from telegraph poles, where dogs bark at the sound of guns in the cold desert darkness, where people vanish in the night. And the nights are long. It's the end of October; the sun sets at six o'clock and will not rise again till seven the next morning. Thirteen hours of darkness in which all manner of evil can bloom, flowers that need no sun.

4

The night is yet to come.

It's still warm. The truck cannot yet be heard, and on the corner of Rancho Anapra and Tiburón, where the paving stops and the road runs off toward the North as dirt, kids are playing in the street. Here, far from the ocean, where water is so precious, nearly all of the streets have the names of fish. On Tiburón, the shark, a little girl and her friends watch her big brother wheeling his bike around in circles by the hardware store, showing off. Another group hangs out by the twenty-four-hour automated water kiosk, hoping to beg a few pesos to buy some bottles. A gaggle of parents coming back from a workshop at Las Hormigas passes by, talking about what it means to be better mothers, better fathers.

Then there's Arturo. Almost invisible, he steers his way steadily along Rancho Anapra. He glances at the kids. So serious. So seriously they play, that as Arturo weaves between them, they have no idea he's even there. There's a smile inside him, a smile for their seriousness, and on another day he might have joked with them a little and made them laugh, but he's too tired for that today, way too tired. Some days he helps out in an auto shop and this is one of those days. He's been lugging old tires around the yard all afternoon and his shoulders ache from the effort of that while his brain aches from the effort of listening to José, the owner, complaining.

Cars come and go down the road. A bus stops and a load of maquiladora workers climb out and stand around for a while, chatting. A patrol car crawls by, a rare enough sight in Anapra. The factory workers see the car and begin to disperse into the streets of fish, but they needn't worry, the cops are just thirsty. One of the cops gets out and wanders over to the water shop. He buys a couple of bottles and heads back to the car, ruffling the hair of one of the boys. He doesn't give them any money. Handing one of the bottles through the window of his car to his colleague, he pulls the cap off his own. Then, as he tilts his head back to drink, the sound of the pickup comes down the street.

Trucks come and go all the time, but the people know what this is. It's moving fast, it has the growl of a powerful engine. It bowls into sight over the crest of the road and heads rapidly toward them. The people scatter. It might be nothing, but better to be sure. The truck gets closer; a flashy dark-red body, tinted windows. Two guys in the cab, another four clinging on in the bed.

As if trying not to disturb the air, the cop carefully gets back in his patrol car and nods to his colleague, just as the truck reaches them, slowing right up, dropping to a crawl as it passes. All six men stare at the cops, who make very, very sure that they do not look back.

Everyone else has disappeared.

Arturo too looks for somewhere to vanish, and quickly backs into the shaded doorway of a green house on the corner opposite, an unusual house, one of the very few with more than one floor. The four men climb down from the bed and, pulling out pistols, head into the hardware store. The policemen start their car and drive steadily away, back toward the city.

Arturo doesn't feel that frightened; this is, God knows, not something new, but suddenly he feels very visible. He makes himself small in the doorway, as small as he can, and stands very still.

The four men are dragging the owner of the shop into the street. The man is called Gabriel. Arturo doesn't really know him, nothing much beyond his name. The men are roughing him up, nothing too serious, but then, as Gabriel tries to fight back, one of them hits him on the side of his head with the heel of a pistol and he slumps to the dust, barely conscious. Arturo can see the blood even from across the street.

The men haul Gabriel into the bed of the pickup, and climb back in, two of them clinging to the sides and two of them lounging on an old sofa that's been bolted to the floor. The truck makes a turn across the median, heading back to Juárez, and Arturo starts to relax, but as it passes him, the driver of the truck looks over and sees him. Their eyes meet. Their eyes meet, and as they do, Arturo feels something jolt, as if the world has shuddered underneath his feet.

The man's face is tattooed, more ink than skin; markings of a narco gang, but at this range it's hard to see which. His head is shaven; he's dressed, as are all the men, in a white wife-beater shirt; tattoos snake all down the muscles of both arms. In slow time, the driver straightens his left arm out of the cab window, and points at Arturo. He makes a pistol with his thumb and forefinger, cocking his thumb back, aiming the gun right at Arturo, who cannot look away as the man drops his thumb, and mouths something, something Arturo cannot grasp.

The man's head tilts back, his mouth open as he laughs. He flattens his foot to the floor and the truck speeds away, back toward the city. The cops are long gone, and anyway, it's not the police these men are scared of; they're scared of the other pandillas, the other gangs, like the M-33, the gang whose turf this is, for now at least.

* * *

It's over. They've left, and the tattooed narco is gone, but Arturo can still feel that finger pointing at him, right at his face, as if the fingertip is pressing into his forehead. It's so strong a sensation that Arturo reaches up and tries to rub it away.

Above him, unseen, something hovers. It is something with immense power. Pure bone, and charcoal eye. Ephemeral yet eternal: the White Girl. The Beautiful Sister. The Bony Lady. Santísima Muerte. Her shroud ripples in the breeze, white wings of death. She holds a set of scales in one hand; in the other, she holds the whole world. Her skull-gaze grinning, her stare unflinching. She looks down at Arturo; she looks down at everyone.

As the truck disappears from view, Gabriel's wife, whose name Arturo does not know, emerges into the street, screaming, her kids clinging to her legs, crying without really knowing why.

—¡Hijos de la chingada!

She screams it over and over.

—¡Hijos de la chingada!

It isn't clear if she means the men who have taken her husband, or herself, her family. One or two people emerge from hiding and rush to give her comfort when there is no comfort to be had.

Far, so very far away, on the other side of the street, Arturo looks down and sees what he has been standing on.

Here, outside the green house, is something strange—a stretch of concrete sidewalk, where everywhere else the sidewalks are dirt. There are marks on the concrete, marks of chalk. They are lines and curves; there are arrows, and small crosses and circles within the curving lines. One device, a pair of interlocking curving arrows, is intersected by seven more arrows that point into the house. So now Arturo realizes where he is, which doorway he has backed into.

Cautiously, he edges away, and looks up at Santa Muerte herself, Saint Death. La Flaquita, the Skinny Lady. She's printed on a plastic banner that's pinned to the wall of the house, right above the doorway. The plastic has been in the full sun for years now; her blacks have become grays, the green globe of the earth is weakened and weary. Above her, in a semicircle, it's still just possible to make out some writing on the fading plastic: No temas a donde vayas que haz de morir donde debes.

Don't worry where you're going; you will die where you have to.

No! She is not the Catrina. She is not that enticing girl of flowers and feathers, that sultry seductress of death. Neither is she the sugary skulls to be eaten, the calaveritas, with the names of the beloved lost. Nor is she the Halloween reaper of gringo fame, scythe in hand, though she could wield it as well as anyone, and does!

No! She is not those impostors, those delusions of decay. For she comes without negotiation. She has no need of come-hither eyes. She is not sugar; she is not candy in the Halloween basket. Yet she is fair. She welcomes all. She opens her arms to the saint and the sinner, to the rich and the poor, to prostitute and narco-lord, to criminal and police chief; a folk saint, a rebel angel, a powerful divinity excommunicated from the Orthodox. She is she, of absolute loyalty. She judges no one, and yet everyone will judge themselves by her in the end.

Yes! She is Santa Muerte, she is Santísima Muerte; the most holy! She is Saint Death. That is who you should worship!

ISLA DE SACRIFICIOS

There, no more than ten meters away, is the fence. Beyond it, is El Norte, where *metros* somehow become *yards*. Thirty of them bring you to the railroad tracks, upon which mile-long freight trains lumber slowly past, night and day, slowly enough to make their contents a target for anyone willing to risk it. Heading in from the west, the twin tracks run parallel to the border, within feet of the fence, until this point. Here, just beyond where Arturo lives on Isla de Sacrificios, lies a hill, Mount Cristo Rey, forcing the American railroad to swing north before it continues its journey east and south around the hill. On the top of the hill Christ himself stands with his arms outstretched, facing both Juárez and, on the other side of the river, El Paso, in a gesture of brotherly love. It's a misleading gesture. His arms are outstretched because he is nailed to a cross.

It's a funny kind of fence. One day, perhaps it will stretch the whole length of the border, almost two thousand miles of it. Right now, less than half has been constructed, from stretches of double-height twin fences with border patrols and searchlights, to single-height runs of chain link. In other places it's three-wire cattle fence, or climb-proof steel plates, or even piles of crushed cars. There are sections of concrete-filled thin wall, and stretches of nothing more than concrete posts in the ground, yards apart from each other. At its western end it trails off into the Pacific Ocean as a series of rusting iron girders poking out of the sand like the fingers of a giant buried robot.

The fact that the fence is not complete is something Arturo is well aware of, because from here, at the corner of Salmón and Isla de Sacrificios, he can see the break in the line. It appears that, faced with the arduous task of climbing Mount Cristo Rey, the fence simply stopped. There is nothing. No border, no line, no concrete marker posts. Nothing. Just a dried-up watercourse coming down from the hill, and Mexican sand, which at some point becomes American sand. Arturo knows this well, for he buries his cooking gear, and any other big stuff that he doesn't want stolen from his shack, out here in the sand, usually choosing a creosote bush as a marker. He guesses he sometimes buries his stuff in America, sometimes Mexico, it doesn't matter to him. What matters is not having his stuff stolen.

It's a funny kind of fence, Arturo thinks, which you can simply walk around. And it's not even as if the hill is insurmountable, for while the peak upon which Christ stands with his arms out is getting on for five thousand feet, its lower slopes are easy going. Besides which, you could drive an army of trucks across the flat patch of desert from the end of the fence to the start of the foothills, just behind Arturo's jacal. That's a funny kind of fence, and one day, Arturo supposes, men will come from El Norte and finish the job, right over the hill to join up with the border again—the great river that runs between El Paso and Juárez. Up to any point before then, Arturo could simply walk into America.

A hundred feet would find him at the railroad tracks. Three thousand feet would get him to New Mexico Route 273. Another three thousand feet, and he could be in Sunland Park, fooling around on the rides at Western Playland. On still evenings, or when the wind blows gently south, he can hear the music blaring from the rides: garish norteño, American pop, or narco-rap lite, not the real stuff, because that might scare people.

On nights like those, when the sound of America comes to him, he lies on the crates he uses for a bed, closes his eyes, and imagines that he's there, with his family who loves him, or friends, or better, a great girl who's crazy about him.

Any night of the year, he could pack up the almost nothing that he owns: a folding knife he likes with a pretty Catrina skull on the handle, a pack of cards for playing calavera, his dirty red Angels cap. He could put on his jacket, and he could go and start a new life.

He doesn't. He never has. People try it, from time to time, and he has thought about it, of course. But he has also thought about the things he hears in the night. Things he hears after Western Playland has gone to sleep.

Sometimes people smugglers walk right past his shack, feet away, hissing instructions to the pollos—the "chickens" hoping for a better life somewhere else. And he hears trucks and Jeeps out in the desert, their engines revving. It's such a cheap-looking piece of sand, in the day. Only at night is it clear that this is very expensive dirt. That this scrubby land is something valuable, and being fought over. This fact is often confirmed by the sounds of voices, shouting, panicking. Gunfire. Single shots from pistols. The repeated stutter of automatic rifles. Arturo sees lights sometimes: floodlights on the Jeeps of narco gangs, the flashing blues and reds of police trucks, the regular cops or Migra, the patrols hunting immigrants. He's heard American voices once in a while, crackling and hissing over radios just yards from where he sleeps, though because he speaks almost no English he never understands.

And everyone has seen the remains of nights like that, the mornings after. Kids come and stand around the bodies, looking on in the way that only little kids can, looking on blankly, understanding nothing. Arturo remembers one morning when he saw a gaggle of children standing around the remains of a necklacing: someone executed by a burning tire forced around their chest and arms. The kids just stared, until their mothers arrived. Then they stood and looked too.

It could be something elaborate like that, it could be just a single bullet; either way, these are the things that happen in the desert at night.

And is it better, Arturo has wondered, to be a fly who spends the whole of its short life banging against a closed window, buzzing crazy, buzzing, buzzing until its life runs out and it drops to the windowsill, slowly twitching, or to be a fly who finds an opening, a gap in the window frame, and flies out to who knows where? Who knows what?

Arturo pulls his grimy T-shirt off and drops it on the dirt floor, then lies on his bed. His shoulders ache so badly they burn. He feels nothing else, can think of nothing else, but slowly, eventually, his body eases, and with it, his thoughts turn outside of himself. José was in fine form today; within five minutes he managed to complain both about the heat and the fact that winter is coming, something Arturo is equally well aware of. Already the nights are cold, and he will have to find an extra blanket or two somewhere. He has a kind of stove he made from an empty oil drum and a length of plastic pipe for a chimney, which pokes through his roof. Most of the time he has little to burn on it, and even when he does, it doesn't work very well. On the rare occasions he does get it fired up strongly, the plastic pipe is liable to melt and toxic black smoke churns into the room, choking him. There are holes in the corrugated tin that's stretched over his packing crate roof, and he could do with fixing it on a little better too. Nails driven through bottle caps make cheap rivets, but they wear loose in the end.

He should cook something. Soon. He should get up and get a drink. He doesn't. He's thinking about Gabriel, at the ironmonger, wondering what he'd done, though he knows that's a stupid thing to wonder. No one deserves to be dragged out of their home in broad daylight, taken away from their family. But he'd done something—said something, been somewhere, just plain *done* something that someone else with guns didn't like. He might show up again, but Arturo doubts it. And if he does show up, he'll show up dead. The best to be hoped for is that it will be a swift ending.

He can forget Gabriel, and he does, quickly, because he's seen it often enough, but he cannot forget that narco, the one driving the pickup, pointing an imaginary gun at him, mouthing something at him, mouthing something, but what? He tries to replay it in his head to see if he can see the words falling from his lips, but he can't. All he can see is the half-tattooed face, laughing, laughing, laughing, and all he can feel is that fingertip, pressing into his forehead, hard.

We are alone, everywhere!

Everywhere alone, and our solitude is all the greater for the knowledge that we have been abandoned in the wide desert of the world, abandoned by uncaring gods, deaf to our cries and blind to our devotions.

We, the people of these gods, we are torn from the womb of the world, and so, desperate for reunion, we wander. We have wandered far from the dark caves where once we huddled around a fire, for warmth, for protection. Hermanos. And wandering far, or staying near, one thing alone is true: each of us dies the death he is looking for.

LA HORA DE LA HORA

I want to destroy something, Arturo thinks, as he lies on his bed. And if I cannot destroy something, then I want to create something. It's time. It's time.

He gets no further than this, does not begin to unravel the logic of these illogical thoughts, for as he stares at the ceiling, he hears a car outside. A car outside is not enough to draw his attention; what draws his attention is that the car has stopped, right outside his shack.

Still lying down, he lifts a corner of cardboard where it has come free from the packing crate wall. The only person he knows with a car is José. He has four or five beat-up old wrecks, only one of which will be working at any given time, and this car, which has stopped outside, is not one from his boss's current collection. It's a white Ford, sunk on its heels, almost dead.

Arturo can't make out who's driving it, not at first, but then he sees the door open, and out of it, as if he were here yesterday, steps Faustino.

—¡Cabrón!—says Arturo, under his breath. He sits up, pulling his dirty shirt back on, and then Faustino is already slapping his hand on the roof.

—¡Hey! ¡Chingada! ¿You in there?

Arturo wants to say no. ¡No! I'm not here. ¿And anyway, where the hell have you been all year?

But he doesn't. And the door, which is the door of some old closet and has no lock, is opening.

Faustino steps inside.

—¡Sure, just come on in!—Arturo says, and he tries to say it like he's mad, but then, Jesus, it's Faustino! It's Faustino! And he starts laughing, unable to stop himself.—¡I might have had a girl in here!

Faustino stands there, laughing too.

—First time for everything. ¿Right, cabrón?

Arturo tells him to shut up and then he tells him to come right in and sit down, and Faustino walks over, his hobble just as obvious as it always was, his head nearly scraping the roof. He doesn't sit.

Arturo waves a hand at him.

—¿Have you grown, vato? You were always so skinny.

Faustino stares at Arturo.

Arturo stares at Faustino, wondering who's going to talk about it first. And if it's Faustino, what he's going to say. But Faustino just stands there, like he was here yesterday, like he was here this morning, saying nothing. Arturo can see he's changed. Faustino's wearing a long-sleeved flannel shirt, but the cuffs are rolled up a ways and Arturo can see there are tattoos on his arms. He had no tattoos before. Arturo cannot make out what they are. The shirt looks like it's pretty damn new, and he wears it open over a white T-shirt. And Arturo has noticed the Nike Cortezes on Faustino's feet. Well, he thinks, if you're going to have only one and a half feet, you may as well put them in some fucking fine shoes.

Still, Faustino stands. He stands, and there's something else about him. There's a bigger change than all these clothes, than the fact that he has enough cash to run a car, even if it's a piece of crap.

Arturo sees the earth tremble under Faustino's one and a half feet. His legs plant themselves into the ground as if they go way underground, miles down, so that as he leans forward slightly, ducking under the roof, there is no danger he will fall. He is rooted. Something has erupted, something has given him power. Something from the old land has come to dwell in Faustino, investing him with force, a force so powerful the very ground trembles, the air shakes around him.

Now, the smile slips from Faustino's face, slowly, slowly, and as it does, Arturo's gaze falls on the webbing belt around his old friend's waist. There's a Catrina there, a gaudy Catrina skull for the buckle, grinning back at him.

—Well—says Arturo.—Quite the cholo now. ¿Eh, cabrón? One thing: that buckle is re-gacho.

Faustino's smile is long dead. He takes two strides over and hits Arturo on the side of the head.

Arturo lurches sideways on the bed, more stunned than hurt, at least for now, and stares back at Faustino, who's glaring at him like an animal. Then Arturo throws himself at him and they fight, collapsing into a struggle, scrabbling at each other, as Arturo shouts—¿Where were you, chingada? ¿Where have you been all damn year?

Faustino doesn't answer. They wrestle some more; they fight like little kids, panting hard, arms flailing and fists making bad blows that hurt all the same.

Then Faustino, who's not as skinny as he once was, rolls Arturo onto his back, and as he does, Arturo's hands knock against something heavy and hard on Faustino's back.

An automatic pistol falls onto the dirt floor.

Arturo sees it, and immediately stops struggling. Faustino thumps Arturo once more, but meekly; the fight has gone from them, and so he stops too, and sits up, pushing his hand back through his hair. Arturo stares at the gun, then he stares at his friend.

—¿What the hell?

Faustino doesn't answer. He gets off his friend, picks up the gun and tucks it down the back of his jeans, as if it were the habit of a lifetime. Then he sits on the bed. Then he starts crying.

Arturo has never seen Faustino cry. Not in all their years as brothers in the colonia. Not in all their time, despite everything they've seen, despite everything that's happened to them, Faustino was always the calmer one, always the wiser one.

Arturo doesn't know what to do, what to say. Finally, he thumps his friend's knee with a gentle fist.

—¿Vato, what's wrong?

Faustino's holding his head.

—I'm in trouble. I'm in big trouble. Jodido.

Arturo doesn't say anything.

Now, the world shakes again, but it is not Faustino who is

shaking the world. It is the world shaking him, shaking them both. Deep down in the soil of the desert, deep down in the old rocks of the earth, things that have been true since Man first erected a totem and worshipped it are about to rise out of the ground and swallow them both, unless they can cheat their way out of it, though that will mean cheating truth itself, and meanwhile, the air in the shack vibrates with the buzzing of flies stuck against the walls, trying to escape, trying to find a crack in the cardboard through which to wriggle out.

—¿So? ¿What happened?

Faustino stares at the ground, saying nothing. Arturo sits back on the floor, uneasy.

—Come on, carnal, it can't be so bad.

It's a dumb thing to say. Faustino lifts his head and the look on his face reminds Arturo of a time, long ago. They'd hitched a ride into Juárez, looking for fun, messing around, and at the end of the day they'd climbed onto the roof of a massive warehouse by the railroad tracks. They'd looked out across the whole damn city, and then they'd stood at the edge, daring each other to go closer to the drop. They got closer and closer, urging each other on, calling each other names, until finally, with their toes hanging into space, they'd realized it wasn't a game anymore. That's the look he sees now, on Faustino's face.

Arturo tries again to reach his friend. He gets off the floor and sits next to Faustino on the bed, Faustino, with his new shoes and expensive clothes.

—¿Cabrón, what are you?

—Soy un halcón.

A falcon. His best friend has become a lookout for a gang.

—¡Meirda! ¿Who for?

—There's a new pandilla. Los Libertadores. On the west side of the city. In Chaveña. That's where I live now.

—¿In Chaveña?

Faustino nods, says nothing.

—But falcons are just kids, vato. They don't give guns to—

—I'm not a kid. I—

Arturo cuts him off.

—I was going to say they don't give guns to *falcons*.

—I'm more than a falcon. I run this bunch of kids. The boss gave me a gun. Keep them in order. Know I'm in business. ¿Right? My boys keep an eye on things in the street. They see anything, they tell me and I tell El Carnero.

—¿Who's El Carnero?

—The boss. His real name is Eduardo Cardona, but they call him El Carnero. Because of the way he fights. Like a ram.

Faustino taps the top of his head.

—¿So you work for the cartel?

—¡No! No, cabrón, I'm not dumb. I work for Los Libertadores.

—¿Yeah? ¿And who do they work for?

Faustino hesitates, then mumbles—They're with Barrio Azteca.

—¡And they work for the cartel! You're right. ¡Que esta jodido!

—No, no. That's not the problem. Life's good. I got money. A car.

—¿Yeah? ¿Life's good? ¿So why are you crying like a little kid?

Faustino doesn't even react to the insult. He wipes his face and tries to look Arturo in the eye, but finds he can't, not right now.

—I borrowed some money.

—¿I thought you said you had money?

—I mean serious money. El Carnero gave me a stash to look after. A big stash. I don't know why. I figured he wanted to keep it away from the rest of his gang . . .

—¿And?

—And I borrowed some of it.

—¿How much?

—A thousand.

Arturo stares at Faustino, speechless. It's not possible that this is happening. This is Faustino. This is goofy little Faustino, and they used Anapra as a playground, and yes, the women were going missing then a lot, but Arturo and Faustino were just little kids and they still found a way to be little kids, despite all the disappearances, and all the horror. Now Arturo realizes something, something his friend didn't say . . .

—¿You mean pesos, right? A thousand pesos.

Faustino shakes his head and Arturo feels the horror rising inside him.

—¿Dollars?—Arturo asks, his voice lifting.—¿You borrowed a thousand gringo dollars from your jefe? ¿And he gave it to you?

—He doesn't know I took it.

—You're dead.

—I know.

—¿So why did you do it?

—Never mind that. I took the money because I needed it. I really needed it. And I thought I had time to get it back. I could have done that; there are things you can do.

Arturo doesn't want to know what he means by that, but there's no time to wonder anyway; Faustino is still talking.

—El Carnero said he'd come for his stash in two weeks. That was a week ago.

—¿So?

—So I got a message this morning. He's coming for it tomorrow. I don't have it, vato. I don't have it. And he's coming tomorrow night, some time after nine. There's something else.

—¿What?

—I think the whole deal was a setup. A test. To see if I could look after the cash. You don't know what he'll do to me if his twenty grand is light.

Arturo shakes his head. He knows as well as anyone what they'll do to Faustino. He's seen them in the street; the bodies. Or hanging from the overpass, with bits missing. Messages cut into their now-dead skin, messages of warning and hate.

—¿Faustino?

Faustino looks up.

—No offense. ¿But what the hell are you doing here? Arturo waves a hand angrily at his shack, and at the nothing that is in it.

—¿Does it look like I have a thousand dollars to give you? You'd be better off asking some of your new rich friends.

—Believe me, I already tried that.

The way he says it, Arturo feels the insult. *Anywhere but here, anywhere but here. Anyone but Arturo.*

—I already asked everyone I can ask without getting killed. That's why I'm here. You have to help me, carnal, you have to help me.

Arturo shakes his head, and mutters under his breath.

—Cabrón.

Faustino nods.

—I know I am. But I'm begging you.

Arturo hangs his head. He gets off the bed, and goes to the unlit gas lamp that hangs off a bent nail in the center of the ceiling. He sits down again next to Faustino and, setting the battered and rusting lamp on his knee, unscrews the base where the gas canister fits. Tucked in around the tiny gap between the canister and the base, Faustino sees pale green money.

—I hide this here—Arturo says.—No one's going to steal this piece of shit.

He slides the money out and then sets the lamp down, flattening the notes, counting them. He hands them to Faustino.

—¿That's it?

—That's it. That's all there is. I promise you. Fifty dollars.

Faustino gives the money back to Arturo.

—That's not why I came.

—¿No? ¿Then why?

Faustino points at the upturned box that is Arturo's table. Sitting on top of it is Arturo's destiny, and it is this destiny that Faustino is pointing at: a pack of cards. A pack of cards for playing calavera.

Arturo understands what he means.

—No. You're joking.

—You can do it. I know you can. That's how you earn your living. ¿Right?

—I play for pesos. Not dollars. Pesos. I play kids on street corners and I go to El Diván and play their dumb dads. For pesos. I *earn my living* by hauling crap for José.

—¿Yeah? ¿And how often do you work there? ¿And how much does he pay you? I know you make more from calavera than you do working for José. There's this game, Arturo. Every night they play at this club in Chaveña. For dollars. Big dollars. I know you can do it. I've won there, sometimes, and you, you're way better than me. You can do it, vato. I know you can do it.

Arturo holds the money out toward Faustino.

—Take it. If you're lucky and you beg hard enough you can find the rest of it by tomorrow.

Faustino shakes his head.

—Keep it. You'll need it to get into the game.

He fishes into his own pocket and pulls out twenty more dollars.

—Here, take this too. It's all the American money I've got.

Arturo shakes his head.

—Forget it, cabrón. I'm not doing it.

—You have to. ¡You have to!

Arturo stands, backing away, shouting.

—¡No, I don't have to! You didn't have to come here. You didn't have to come and ask for my help. ¡Last year you drop out of my life, just like that! You could have been dead. I never heard from you, not once. ¿And then you come back here like it's yesterday and you want me to put my neck in a noose for you? ¡No way! ¡Chingada! ¡No way!

Faustino stands too.

—¡You! ¡You're a dreamer! ¡Stupid! ¿You think we're still kids? ¿You think we don't grow up? Things change, vato, things change.

—Yeah, I can see that.

Arturo looks at his friend, at his clothes, the shoes, the tattoos. Even his haircut says he is not who he once was.

—You think you're some kind of big man, now. ¿Is that it?

—I'm not a kid anymore, Arturo. I'm not a kid.

—¿And when did that happen?—Arturo shouts.—¿When they gave you a gun?

That hits Faustino. He says nothing for a moment, runs his hand across his slicked-back hair. Then he points at Arturo, stabbing the air.

—No—he says.—It happened when I stopped thinking about myself and started thinking about other people.

He says it quietly, so quietly it takes the anger out of Arturo. He too stands for a long time without saying anything, his chest heaving, his breath slowing as he calms down, and he thinks about what Faustino just said and he knows that it's way too smart for Faustino to have thought of it and wonders who it is who put that idea in his head.

Then Arturo says—No. I won't do it. I'm sorry, Faustino. I don't want to die.

—You won't. There's no risk for you. At worst you lose your dollars. They won't know you have anything to do with me.

But Arturo shakes his head.

Faustino slams his hand against the wall of the shack. The whole thing shakes, and then this brief anger is gone too.

—Come here.

He goes to stand by the door, pushes it open.

—I said, *come here.*

Arturo comes over and steps outside after Faustino, who calls out, to the car.

Now Arturo realizes that there is someone else in the car, someone he couldn't see before. The passenger door opens and out steps Eva.

In her arms, she's holding a bundle. The bundle makes a noise, a little cry.

Faustino puts his hand on Arturo's shoulder, and with the other hand points at Eva and the baby.

—You're not doing it for me. You're doing it for them.

At 3.54 p.m, 11/6/16, CHOMSKY68 wrote:

Should there even be border controls?

Crazy, you say?

Say you believe in a free market. Nobody actually does, but say you're one of those people who claim to believe in free markets. Well, free markets are supposed to be based on the free movement of labor. No free movement of labor, no free markets, right? But nobody talks about that.

So should there be border controls? Should people be free to live and work where they want, where the market "wants" them to? It depends on what you think countries are for.

It's an interesting question to ask in a country where (unless you're a native) everyone is an immigrant. The native peoples didn't have the power to stop immigrants coming in.

Now we're trying to stop anyone else getting in.
In the end, it's all about power. Wealth, and power.

FAUSTINO RIDES THE BEAST

Tomorrow is the word. *Tomorrow* was always the word, for Faustino. Arturo looks from his old friend to Eva.

Eva is jiggling her hip up and down, trying to soothe her baby, who's started grizzling. She lifts a hand and gives Arturo a little wave, a weak smile.

Automatically, Arturo raises his hand in reply, and then he turns back to Faustino again, because Faustino is asking him something.

—¿You want to see him? ¿My little boy?

Arturo knows now they've stopped being kids. He just can't work out when that happened. He doesn't answer Faustino, doesn't move, he just stares at Eva and the baby, until eventually he says—¿What's going on?

Faustino shrugs.

—I guess tomorrow finally came.

Tomorrow, tomorrow, tomorrow.

It was Faustino's word before he and Arturo even met. It was his father's word even before Faustino was born. Back home, in Guatemala, his father used to say it to his mother: tomorrow I will get a job. Tomorrow I will mend the roof. Tomorrow everything will be okay. And Faustino's mother would roll her eyes and moan and love her husband anyway. They survived in La Limonada, picking scraps from the garbage dump, reselling what they could, along with sixty thousand other people crammed into the teetering ravine that cuts almost to the heart of Guate.

One day, Faustino was born, and then his father taught him the word too; tomorrow we'll go to the park and play football, tomorrow I'll find you a bike, tomorrow I'll show you how to ride it.

As Faustino grew, however, something changed in his father, and the word changed too. It actually began to mean something, and finally, one day, Faustino's father said to Faustino's mother—We cannot stay here anymore.

It wasn't just the poverty. It wasn't just the murders, the police who did nothing, who wouldn't even enter La Limonada. It wasn't just the floods and the landslides. It wasn't just the outbreaks of disease. It was all of these things and more that one day made Faustino's father say to Faustino's mother—Tomorrow we will go to America.

This time, when he said tomorrow, he meant it. It was bad that he and his wife had lived like this for ten years, but he couldn't let the same thing happen to their only child.

One day, just before Faustino's seventh birthday, they left. They had sold everything they had, for dollars where they could. They had been saving what little they earned. It was now or never.

They knew where to go; everyone told stories about people

who'd made it, and everyone knew the dangers too, but despite that they hitched a ride north to the border with Mexico. At Tecún Umán they paid a lanchero ten dollars to cross the Suchiate River on his makeshift raft of planks lashed to giant inner tubes. It should have cost them only a dollar, but the lanchero could see they weren't locals. He knew what they were, and he knew their desperation had a price. So did the border guard who stopped them almost as soon as they set foot on Mexican soil, in Hidalgo. He searched their bags indifferently; two plastic sacks with everything they had left in the world, explaining that he was looking for drugs, or guns. Finding none, he stuck out a hand for his bribe, and left them to continue their journey.

They were lucky. They made it to Tapachula in one piece, grabbing rides in the backs of trucks for another few dollars each time. No one assaulted them. No one robbed them. No one beat Faustino's father or raped Faustino's mother. No one dragged Faustino away into the bushes.

In Tapachula they asked around and got directions to the Casa del Migrante, a shelter run by a middle-aged Italian priest. Aside from a small rosary around his neck, he looked more like the owner of a bar than a man of the cloth. He spoke dirty, mestizo Spanish, with Italian thrown in here and there, but he gave them, and dozens of others, a bed for two nights and hot meals. He prayed for them, and he handed them pamphlets about the dangers of the road ahead, which they politely took and then did not read.

They chewed their food, and they waited for their time to come.

Faustino spent much of this time staring at one wall of the

shelter, to which was pinned a large, grubby map, with graffiti and other scrawlings all over it.

—¿What is it, Papá?

Faustino's father pointed out some places.

—That's Guate, where we came from. That's where you were born, niño. And that's where we are now. Here, in Tapachula.

Faustino kept staring.

—¿How far is that?

—Three hundred kilometers.

—¡That's so far!—said Faustino.—¡We must be nearly in Los Angeles!

Faustino's father didn't smile. How could he tell his son that they had barely begun? How could he tell him there were over four thousand kilometers more still to travel? He could not.

After their two nights, they left the shelter along with the priest's blessing and twenty-two other men and women. There were a few kids on the trail north, but none as young as Faustino. People looked at his parents and some muttered and some even told them it was crazy to bring a young boy along.

It was almost another three hundred kilometers to Arriaga, and they walked some of the way, and took buses when they could, though they knew that if anyone asked for their papers they would be detained and deported back to Guatemala, and still they were lucky. Along the way, Faustino listened to what the grown-ups were saying, who spoke as adults always do, as if children cannot hear. But Faustino did hear, and he heard one word, over and over again: la bestia. The beast.

The beast, the beast, the beast, until finally, Faustino grew scared of it. He picked up on not just what they were saying, but how they said it, and as it is so often, though children do not *know*, they understand anyway. And he understood; the beast was something of which to be afraid.

—¿Papá?—he asked.—¿What is the beast?

His father looked at his mother, and his mother shrugged, and so his father explained.

—Tomorrow, Faustino, we will ride the beast. The beast is huge. ¡A kilometer long! ¡Longer! And the beast will take us to America.

Still, Faustino did not understand, but that evening they arrived in Arriaga, and walked the short way to the railroad station, to the freight terminus, where hundreds of people were settling down for the night, huddling against huts, sleeping between the rails, a ribbon of steel for a pillow. Others simply lay on the ground, in twos or threes, waiting.

Faustino's father was wrong. They did not ride the beast the next day, because the beast did not show. So they waited, and waited, and it was hard to understand what everyone was doing here, hanging around a deserted railroad station, a station with no trains, nor signs posted as to when one might appear.

On the afternoon of the second day, some people came, all wearing orange shirts with the letters GB on them, which no one understood the meaning of, but they handed out water bottles, and warned anyone who would listen about the beast, and the dangers of riding it.

—*Do not climb on a moving train. They may seem slow, but it's too dangerous.*

—Look out for thieves. They may get on the train disguised as migrants like you.

—Look out for Migra.

—When you reach the north, it will be hot. Be careful with your water. The heat can get to 50 degrees Celsius, or more. Higher. It can kill you.

Then, on the second night, it came. At three in the morning, the world began to shake. Deep underground, fantastic leviathans from ancient times were stirred as the tracks vibrated. They forced their way to the surface, gasping for breath, and then the creatures emerged into the fetid night air of southern Mexico and from around the bend in the forest, three dazzling eyes blinded Faustino with light.

—¡Papá!—he cried.—¡The beast!

With no more warning than that, it had come: a train a kilometer long. A freight train, with no passengers or passenger cars, just wagon after wagon of closed steel boxes.

When Faustino saw it was a train, he was no less amazed, no less disappointed than if a dragon had scuttled up from some primeval chasm. It slowed to a crawl and then stopped, and many people shouted and ran and clambered up the steel ladders to the roofs of the boxcars, while others sat on the ground, those who'd made the journey before, who knew it would be hours before the train left again.

The hours passed, and Faustino was scared. He and his mother and father had found a spot under the sloping end of a wagon made to hold liquid goods. It was lower to the ground, and there would be some shelter if it rained. They were joined by three other men and a young woman, none of whom spoke, and Faustino was scared, in this time of waiting; a desperate kind of tension hung all about them, as they waited for someone to come and tell them to get down, or arrest them, or worse. But no one did, and there was no one in sight, no one from the railroad, or the town. Somehow, after hours had passed, during which they ate the last of the food they had, the beast began to move again all by itself, a metal animal, rumbling its way north through the southern Mexican jungles.

—¡That's it!

Faustino's father laughed.

His wife held his hand, clinging to it tightly.

—El Norte. We are going to America, Faustino. ¡Los Angeles!

—¿When, Papá?—asked Faustino.—¿When? ¿Tomorrow?

One of the other men huddling with them laughed. The young woman turned her head away, stared out at the black jungle night.

—No, Faustino. Not tomorrow. But soon.

Faustino spent his seventh birthday clinging to the back of the wagon, huddled between his mother and his father as the rain lashed down. When the rain stopped they passed a village where kind people threw fruit up for them to catch, and they each ate an orange, eating the peel too, licking their fingers clean.

Their luck held still, for a day, and halfway into another night, and then it ran out.

They were asleep, despite the thumping of the train over every crossing, despite the terrible roar that the beast's wheels made on the tracks, despite the colder nights. There were shouts, shouts from ahead on the roof of the train.

—¡Migra! ¡Migra!

—¡Run!

—¡Get off and run!

Confusion swept down the length of the train, as their luck fled faster than they could. For it was not the migration police, but something worse, a gang of robbers. A couple of shots sounded, the gunfire flashed in the dark, and people began to scramble and jump from the train.

Faustino's father shouted at his wife to jump. He had to shout twice. It wasn't far but the dark made it even more frightening. Then Faustino jumped, his wide eyes seeing nothing. Then Faustino's father jumped, and before they knew what was happening, rough hands grabbed them all and lined everyone up in the headlights of a pickup.

Men with guns went along the line and took everything. Money, phones, nice clothes. Everything. They took the young woman, and Faustino's mother, and bundled them into the back of a beat-up van, which sped away as soon as the doors were closed. They shot Faustino's father as he tried to stop all this from happening.

They left Faustino clinging to the body of his dead father in the middle of nowhere, in the middle of the night. After a day passed, even the young Faustino knew he had to move. He waited for the next beast to roll along the tracks, and he tried to climb onto it as it was moving.

Hands reached for him, friendly hands.

—¡Mierda, he's just a kid!

—¡Grab hold, kid! ¡Grab hold!

Faustino tried to grab, but he slipped. His right foot went under the wheel of the train, which sliced it in half. He lay in the dark, unconscious from pain, and his blood flowed and flowed but finally stopped, just before death came.

In the morning, a farmer found him and took him.

Many tomorrows passed. Tomorrows that became months, that became years. Faustino was passed from place to place. He ended up in a hostel for people like him who'd lost a limb, or more, to the beast, but he didn't like it. One day, he begged a middle-aged couple who were heading north to take him with them, and finally, he ended up in Anapra.

He was ten years old.

Somehow, he survived in Anapra. He met Arturo. They became friends. They were brothers, and they even went to school for a short time, which was where they met Eva. And all the time, all the time, Faustino would say to Arturo—Tomorrow, carnal. Tomorrow, I'm going to America. I don't have to stay here. In this dump. I can leave whenever I want. Anytime. ¿You know?

—Yeah—Arturo would reply.—I know, sure.

Tomorrow.

¿What have we done? ¿What have we done?

INSATIABLE GODS

Just like in a game of calavera, Arturo knows that Faustino has played an unbeatable card. The game is won. The game is won because Faustino isn't talking about himself.

Arturo knows Faustino's story, or most of it. He knows what he means when he says "tomorrow." He knows it never really meant anything, not till now. But now that it does mean something, Faustino isn't suggesting *he's* going to leave for America.

—It's Eva—he says.—Eva and the baby. I paid for them to cross.

Arturo can't believe it.

—¿A thousand? I'll hold your hand and we can walk over there right now, cabrón. ¡There it is! ¡Right there! ¡El Norte!

—You're so dumb, vato. You don't just walk into America without a plan. You know that. I paid coyotes to get her to LA. They leave tonight. It would have been five hundred but they wanted an extra five hundred for the baby. I said, no way, it's nothing. It's so small. But they said it could cry and make a noise and get them all caught. Said I was lucky they didn't want a thousand just for the damn kid.

Something's not right.

—Five hundred each—Arturo says.—That's damn cheap. I heard it cost ten times that to keep a coyote happy. I heard it costs five thousand. Or more. ¿No?

Faustino doesn't answer. Arturo knows he knows the answer to the question; he just doesn't want to admit it. But there's Faustino, staring at the ground, looking for all the world like a little kid with his hand caught right in the cookie jar. And Arturo knows exactly why the coyotes are charging a tenth of what they might.

—She's going to be a burro. That's it. She's going to haul drugs for them. ¿Right?

Faustino doesn't reply. He still stares at the ground. Across the street, by the car, Eva stands, rocking the bundle in her arms, staring north, across the desert. Arturo cannot imagine what is in her mind, or, for that matter, what was in Faustino's.

Arturo keeps his voice down, for Eva's sake, but he cannot keep the anger out of his voice.

—¿What were you thinking? Making her a burro . . . ¿She's going to have to carry drugs, and the baby?

Faustino's rage returns. He steps right up to Arturo, hissing into his face.

—I don't have ten thousand dollars, Arturo. I figured I could find a thousand to replace what I took from El Carnero's stash. I knew I couldn't find ten. It was the only way.

Arturo shakes his head.

—You're crazy.

—It was the only way. I had no choice.

It seems there are no answers to Faustino's replies, just as there is no end to his stupidity. Arturo knows it costs a lot to pay a coyote to help you cross over. They promise more than just dumping you in the desert. They have networks of people, to take you to a city, to LA if you can afford it, or maybe Tucson or Phoenix. It costs a lot because the borders are controlled, not just by Migra, not just by the American border patrol. There are other forces controlling who crosses the desert, and you either pay them and be safe, or you take your chances. And even if you do pay them, there are always those cases where they just take you out into the night and—

Arturo stops that thought, dead. Stone dead. Instead, he thinks, ¿Tonight? ¿They're leaving tonight? ¿Eva and the baby?

He puts a hand on Faustino's shoulder.

—¿But you're not leaving?—he asks his friend.

Faustino looks sick. He looks like he will actually be sick on the ground, there and then.

—Listen, I didn't want it this way. Eva's mother threw us out. ¿The moment the baby arrived? She threw us both out. No more mouths to feed, she said. ¡Cabróna! So I said, that's it. We'll go. And I borrowed that money for Eva, but unless I pay it back before tomorrow night, I'm not going anywhere.

—I thought you were the big man now, earning a fortune.

Faustino is rubbing his head, glancing over at Eva from time to time.

—I earn some—he says—but look. That's not what I want. I want out. I don't want to be a falcon. I want Eva and the baby to go to America. And me.

He doesn't say "finally" but Arturo can see the word in his face.

—¿Why didn't you take enough to pay for all of you? You could still go with her. Just run.

Faustino stares at Arturo for a second as if he's crazy, and then he turns and vomits all over the ground.

Arturo takes a step back. Over at the car, Eva wrinkles her nose, and turns away slightly, bouncing the baby.

Faustino stands, bends again, takes a deep breath, then stands and wipes his mouth with the back of his hand.

—Wait—says Arturo, and ducks into his shack. He comes back with a Coke can with the top cut off and tape around it to cover the sharp edge. It's full of water scooped out of the old oilcan Arturo uses to store it.

Faustino takes a swig, spits, throws the rest over his face. He rolls up his left sleeve, wipes his face with his forearm.

—Thanks, carnal. The water here still tastes like shit.

—You're welcome.

Arturo knows that what he said was crazy. Faustino cannot run away. He must settle his debts in Juárez, one way or the other, or there can be no escape. Los Libertadores, the gang he works for, work for Barrio Azteca. They work for the cartel. Both Barrio Azteca and the cartel have people everywhere. In Mexico, in the north. In El Paso, in Los Angeles. As far away as Chicago. In fact, in pretty much every big city. And they don't forget and they don't leave a score unsettled, for these men are gods, insatiable gods, more brutal perhaps than those of the old world, who have lain unappeased in the earth for centuries since they were seemingly overthrown. Only seemingly, for they have not vanished altogether. If Faustino runs, it will be suicide. Delayed suicide, perhaps, but suicide nonetheless.

Now that Faustino has rolled up his left sleeve, Arturo can see one of his tattoos. Two long Ls, interlocked, running down the length of his left forearm. Los Libertadores. His gang, marked on his body, forever. It would be easier, and cheaper, and safer, to get a fake passport than to get that mark taken off. There is nowhere Faustino can run. If he ever wants to sleep again, if he ever wants to spend a day without being scared again, if he ever wants to see Eva again, he must find that money before tomorrow night. If he doesn't, he's already seen enough of what they do to punks like him to know it will not be fast and it will not be easy.

—Okay—says Arturo.—Okay. I'll do it.

Whenever I dream of a closed space, a darkened room, I know I am dreaming of my mind. That the dark space I'm dreaming of represents the world of my mind.

Last night I had such a dream, and I was standing in a big garage, with no cars in it, but I was living in it, or working there, or trying to work there. The doors were open and it was bright outside, but the brightness didn't come into my space.

There were candles hanging from the ceiling on strings, and I was walking around trying to light them with a box of matches, but the matches either broke or didn't light properly, or the candles lit for a moment and then died.

I couldn't light a fire in my head. There were figures in the bright doorway; dark beings in silhouette who were going to come in, and I couldn't light the fire in my head, the light that would keep them away. And as I woke I knew it wasn't just my head: it was the whole city. It was Anapra, it was Juárez, it was all of Mexico. It was the world.

VOICES

Faustino cannot speak. He throws his arms around Arturo, who stands still, who does not put his arms around Faustino, who just waits for him to let go, and step back.

Then Arturo says—Save it for her, vato.

They look over at Eva.

—¿You going to come and say hello?—asks Faustino—¿And goodbye?

Arturo shrugs.

—Sure.

—You never got on with her. Not even when we were kids.

—That's not true—Arturo says.

—Sure it is—says Faustino, laughing.—Even when we were at school. ¿You remember that day Doña Margarita wanted us all to put a handprint and our name on the wall outside? And Eva said something and you smeared paint all over hers.

—And then she poured paint all over my head. Yeah. I remember.

He remembers that, and how mad Doña Margarita, their teacher, was. Not just with him, but with all of them, though not for long. There was a good woman, Arturo thinks, as they walk over to the car, a really kind woman.

Eva turns. My God, thinks Arturo as he sees her. She looks rough. No, not that. She looks . . . older. Eva has aged years since he last saw her. And it's not just the baby in her arms, or the clothes she's wearing. It's not just the makeup or her hair. It's in her face, it's in her eyes, her eyes. Her eyes have aged. She looks . . . tired.

—Hey, Arturo.

—Hey, Eva.

Arturo doesn't ask to look at the baby, and Eva doesn't offer.

—Good luck in El Norte—he says, and she nods.

—Thanks. Good luck to you too.

She glances over his shoulder at his shack. She doesn't mention the game, she doesn't talk about the mess Faustino has got them all into, because to Eva's way of thinking, life is a mess, all the time.

—¿You know people in LA?—Arturo asks.

—My cousin has a friend who made it. I have her telephone number.

All three stand by the car, and no one can think of anything more to say, anything that is worth saying.

Eventually, Faustino opens the door for Eva, who slides back in, holding the baby on her lap.

Faustino shuts the door and walks around to the driver's side.

—I'll be back at seven. I gotta take Eva to the place the

coyotes told us. Then I'll be back. Drive you to the game. ¿Seven, okay?

He gets in the car.

By eight, Faustino has still not returned.

Arturo watches the sun set and the shadows that lengthen across America are the same ones that lengthen across Anapra. A stray dog trots by, its tongue lolling out of its mouth. Arturo knows it. It's often hanging around because he feeds it scraps sometimes. The dog heads toward Arturo for a second, until he throws a handful of dirt at it and it scampers away.

—Not now, vato—he whispers.—I have to think.

In truth, there is nothing much to think about. He's been sitting on a box outside the front of his shack since seven, holding his calavera pack tightly in his hand. There is nothing to think about; nothing to practice, nothing to learn. Calavera is a simple game, really. He only has to keep calm. He has some idea about what he is heading into, and he wishes he knew more and he wishes he knew less. In the meantime, he knows he must keep calm, and when the time comes he must play his usual game, yet all he can really think is, Damn Faustino, damn Faustino, damn Faustino.

The sun has set and it is getting dark. There are few streetlights in the backwaters of a place like Anapra. Arturo ducks back into his shack and hides his playing cards under his mattress. He thinks about making something to eat but doesn't feel hungry. He lies on his bed, thinking, Damn Faustino, damn Faustino, damn Faustino.

My friend. My brother. *Mi carnal.*

At quarter after eight, unable to bear the waiting any longer, Arturo puts on his favorite shirt, an old and fading purple thing that he loves for reasons he could not name even if pressed. He sticks the dollars as deep into his pocket as they will go, the fifty of his own, the twenty Faustino added to it. He sticks Catrina in his other pocket. He slips his rosary over his head, scrapes his hair back with some oil, and goes outside and starts to walk down Salmón, hoping to meet Faustino as he comes.

Lights burn in homes made of cardboard and plywood. A gentle wind shushes the straggling leaves of Anapra's few trees. Voices come and go through the darkness. Voices calling out, laughing. He hears someone crying. He can make out few actual words, but he knows these are the voices of his brothers and sisters, his friends, his enemies and haters. They agree, they disagree. They fight. They love. They all drift in and want to be heard, forcing their way between the leaves on the trees and between the leaves in his head.

Lights blind him. A car pulls up and stops abruptly.

—Get in—says Faustino.

Arturo climbs in.

—You're late, cabrón—says Arturo.

Faustino doesn't reply. He stares through the windshield at the dirt road, doesn't even glance at the place he used to call home till he moved in with Eva's mother in Chaveña.

On Rancho Anapra, Faustino turns right, not left.

—Hey—says Arturo, pointing—Juárez is that way.

Still Faustino says nothing.

Arturo is about to speak when, at the corner of Tiburón, Faustino stops the car.

—¿What are we doing here?

—We need all the help we can get.

Arturo shakes his head.

—¿What are you talking about?

Faustino points to the house on the corner. The green house, with two stories. The one with Santa Muerte hanging over the doorway.

—¿What? No way. ¿What do you want in there?

—She'll help us, vato. And we both need all the help we can get.

—Yeah. ¿But you don't believe in that, do you?

Faustino rolls up his right sleeve. It's hard to make it out in the dark but Arturo can see the other tattoo now, and there's just enough light to see what's been etched there in dark-blue ink: La Dama Poderosa, la Hermana Blanca. The Powerful Lady, the White Sister. A skeleton in a shawl holding the world in her hand.

—I'm not going—begins Arturo but Faustino leans over and grabs the rosary necklace. On the end, Christ dangles on his cross next to the Virgin of Guadalupe.

—¿And you believe in them? ¿Do you? ¿You believe in them? ¿What did they ever do for you? ¿For us?

Arturo shoves him away, but Faustino is still gripping the rosary, which breaks. Beads scatter over the seat and floor of the car, but Faustino does not apologize, does not yield. It appears that the anger in him is relentless, and Arturo is quite simply amazed, *amazed* that Faustino is so angry, because he was never angry before. Never. He was the calm one, he was the peacemaker. Always.

—¡Nothing!—Faustino shouts. ¡They did nothing for us! ¡But she—he says, pointing at the house—she is powerful! And she welcomes everyone. Everyone.

He shoves the remains of the rosary into Arturo's hands.

—Keep them—he says.—But if you want real help, come with me.

Faustino gets out of the car and slams the door. He goes to the house, where he pushes a bell.

After a wait, the door opens a crack and light floods out. Arturo watches as Faustino starts talking, sees him waving his hand back toward the car, and then the door opens fully.

A woman steps into the street, right where Arturo cowered earlier in the day when the men took Gabriel. She's short and round. She's waving at Arturo, gently beckoning, and smiling.

—Come—she calls.—Come into my home.

She waves again, and smiles.

So Arturo goes in.

A VISIT TO THE HOUSE OF DEATH

Arturo and Faustino wait in the hall.

The woman, who is not as old as Arturo thought at first, has gone to the kitchen. She told Arturo to call her Doña Maria, asked him if he would like coffee, and then went to fix it.

As he came into the house Arturo was careful to step over the strange chalk marks on the sidewalk. The arrows and the curved lines.

—¿What are those things, vato?—he asks Faustino in a whisper.—Those things outside. ¿Some sort of magic?

—Doña Maria said they let good spirits in and keep bad ones out. They're called patipemba, something like that. Old African magic, but that's okay. The White Girl welcomes everyone to her church. Everyone. You'll see.

—¿You've been coming here?—asks Arturo.—¿You've been coming here and not coming to see me?

Faustino at least looks guilty this time. His anger seems to have waned inside Doña Maria's house, and a middle-aged woman's house is all it seems to be. It doesn't look weird, or evil, or anything like Arturo imagined it might. He knows a little about Santa Muerte, because everyone does. He knows she spread up from the south, from Mexico City, maybe, or farther. A saint of the people, not one the Church likes much, that's for sure. And people tell all sorts of tales about her. Lots of it good, but then, Arturo's heard some bad things too. He knows many people worship her. All sorts of people. Drug lords, cops, the poor, the rich. All sorts of people. He just had no idea Faustino was one of them.

Arturo tugs Faustino's sleeve.

—¿So you don't believe in God anymore?

—Sure I do—says Faustino.—I believe in God. But I trust in Santa Muerte.

He doesn't say what he trusts her to do, but Arturo understands. Help. Isn't that all everyone wants? A little help. A guiding hand. Some goddamn luck, once in a while . . .

Doña Maria is coming back, with two mugs of coffee, steaming and black.

—You know the way, Faustino—she says.—You go ahead. I have housework to do.

Arturo takes the coffee readily, thanking Doña Maria, and Faustino leads the way while she disappears back toward the kitchen, from where a radio is blasting harsh voices. A phone-in show, a local one. The voices talk about their lives in Juárez, and as Arturo follows Faustino into the next room he hears a woman weeping about her daughter, and it was just another levantón, she says, another "lift," another "ride." Another "disappearance," that's all it was to anyone else. But to her it was her daughter. The host of the show curses and says he feels her pain, and then he cuts to the next set of advertisements.

Arturo and Faustino stand in the dark room, looking to where, at the far end, something glows. They're in an area that feels as if it's half in the house and half outside. The walls are bare cinder blocks, the floor concrete. It has no windows, save for a small one with a grille in a door that Arturo guesses leads outside. There are a couple of old sofas, some wooden chairs around a table, where he sets the coffees down. But at the far end of the room is what dominates, what emanates power. Arturo sees little else; his eye is drawn to the figure standing on a low table placed in the middle of the far wall. She radiates.

Holy Death. Santa Muerte.

Her bony face, her bony hands.

Arturo stares; her black eyeless sockets stare back.

Arturo blinks. She does not.

She's wearing a white shawl over a long white gown, which reaches to the ground. From under the shawl glimpses of a black wig can be seen, grotesque against the skull face, almost ridiculous, Arturo thinks, and yet it's more disturbing than it is funny, and in a way disconcerting because it is somehow comical too, and do not laugh at death, he thinks, we do not laugh at death.

Her arms are slightly outstretched. In her right hand is a scythe, and in her left, a bunch of rosaries, hanging.

—Come on, vato—says Faustino, and they approach the saint.

Now that they are closer, Arturo sees that she is made of papier mâché, painted with thick white paint. Arturo finds that she is no less convincing for this. The low table she's standing on is an old

TV console, chipped and stained. It's covered in all sorts of things: offerings; candles, lots of candles, many of which are lit, the source of the glow that illuminates her. There are glasses of water. Flowers in bunches and single stems. Loose cigarettes. A joint or two. Scratch cards. There are lots of pieces of paper on the table, under candles, on the walls behind, and pinned to her gown itself. One of the pieces of paper is large, the writing scrawled big enough to read from where they stand.

Abre nuestros caminos para la llegada del dinero.

Open our roads for the arrival of money.

The money seems already to have arrived; there are notes of all kinds, mostly pesos but some dollars too, tucked under candles, in little pots, rolled up and shoved between her fingers of paper-bone.

Arturo cannot fully take his eyes off Santa Muerte; he cannot fully look at her either. Either way, she is there, watching, as he whispers to Faustino.

—¿What is this place, cabrón? ¿Some sort of church?

—It's Doña Maria's shrine. She lets people come and worship, because hers is one of the best in all of Juárez. They leave her offerings. And don't say *cabrón* in here.

Arturo ignores that. He looks around. On the other walls are gaudy paintings, cheaply done, in heavy frames. One shows the Virgin of Guadalupe, another shows Jesús Malverde with his slicked-back black hair and neat black mustache. He's wearing a beige shirt and black bandanna around his neck, and there's a halo behind his head. A third painting shows Christ in agony on the cross. A fourth shows Saint Jude, patron saint of lost causes. Dirty saints, all of them. All of them from the streets. A fifth is not a painting but a poster, nor is it a depiction of a saint, but a huge image of a large Catrina—sexy and lascivious, her black eyes and her skeletal features painted on, small red roses and hearts across her forehead, alluring and menacing all at once. Just like the one on the handle of Arturo's knife.

He turns back to Faustino.

—¿And you come here?

Faustino doesn't answer.

He goes up to the figure and kneels, picks up the hem of her gown and kisses it.

He stands, and fumbling in his pockets pulls out a bent cigarette and a disposable lighter. He lights the cigarette and begins to puff.

—¿Since when do you smoke, cabrón?—Arturo asks.

—I don't so much—says Faustino.—But *she* does.

With that, he leans right up to her face and blows gentle wreaths of smoke into her gaping skull mouth.

—She likes it—he explains.—She likes all the things we like. ¿You don't believe? ¿See this water? She drinks it. If we come back later she will have drunk the water. She likes beer too, and tequila. I'm giving her a smoke. She'll look after us both tonight. And don't swear in front of her.

Arturo laughs, then stops himself as he sees Faustino's face.

—Show some respect—says Faustino. The cigarette is half burned down. He stubs it out on the bottom of his shoe and leaves it by one of the candles. He comes back to Arturo.

—She helps anyone who asks for help. And we need help. People leave her a little money. She pays them back ten times over. ¡A hundred times! ¿How do you think Doña Maria built this house? She was good to our White Sister and our White Sister has paid her back. She's here to help, vato, and you should get down on your knees and worship her because tonight you're going to need all the help you can get.

Arturo doesn't move. He looks at Faustino, then glances at Santa Muerte, briefly, whose eyeless gaze has never left him, not once, not since he first stepped into the room.

—No—he says quietly.—I can't.

—¡Hijo de puta!

Faustino shoves Arturo in the shoulder, who backs away, holding his hands up for peace. He knows lots of people worship her, all sorts of normal people, and yet something about it makes him uncomfortable. Words drop into his head, words he heard a friend of theirs once say: *When you cross a bridge there is always something to pay*, but Arturo has no idea what it means, not yet, and Faustino is waiting for him to answer.

—I can't do it, Faustino. Don't make me.

—¿You scared? There's nothing to be scared of. She's here to help us. ¿Who else has helped you? ¿Who? ¡No one!

Arturo shrugs. He shakes his head. Faustino curses again.

—You just said not to swear in here—Arturo says.

Faustino laughs.

—Oh, she doesn't mind. Not really. She's one of us. Listen, you have to do it. If not for you, then for me. And if not for me then for Eva.

—¿And the kid?

—And the kid, right.

Arturo hesitates.

Faustino tries to be patient. It's something he used to be very good at, but now it seems to take an enormous effort of will. He takes a deep breath.

—¿Do you know how much Eva made in the maquiladora?

Arturo shakes his head.

—A hundred pesos. A day. A hundred pesos a day. And she had to pay eighteen pesos a day out of that to the company bus to bring her to work in their own damn factory. An American factory, whose managers live in El Paso and come over to Juárez to work and earn twenty, thirty times what Eva did, and in dollars, and then drive back over the Puente Internacional to their nice homes. And they have days off and health care; all that stuff. There's no laws over here for those American factories. Nothing. ¿You know what happened when they found out Eva got pregnant? She lost her job. Just like that. And since then, we would've been screwed, but for one thing.

He points at Saint Death.

—Her. She saved us. She got me my job. And now I have some money and we can buy food and without her we'd be dead. So get down on your damn knees and pray to her, Arturo.

Arturo holds his friend's angry gaze, but it cannot last. He feels Faustino's pain, and it is too much to bear.

He lifts his arms out to the sides. Shrugs.

—¿What do I do?

—Anything you want. Give her something. ¿Do you have anything to give her? Not your dollars, we need your dollars. You can just light a candle for her and ask her for help. She'll listen. She listens to people like us. You'll see.

61

Arturo still hesitates. But Faustino is waiting, staring at him, and she is waiting, staring at him. She could wait forever. So Arturo gets down on his knees, on the bare concrete, and bows his head.

He mumbles something, quietly, so that Faustino cannot hear. He lifts his head, and looks at the table before him. Dozens of people have been here before him. Some have left notes. Now that Arturo is closer he can read some of them, even the old ones, very old and faded, those that speak of the missing of Juárez. The girls, the women.

Bring her back safe.

Protect her, wherever she is.

Bring her back to us. O holy death, bring her back.

Countless women who were taken by the gangs. And by the police, and by the army, who were able to pass off anything as the work of the narcos, and besides, as everyone knows, it's hard to tell just where the gangs stop and the cops start.

The disappeared women. Most of them never seen again, and those that were seen again . . . It's better not to think of that, Arturo knows. He looks at the notes left by people who believed that Santa Muerte could help them, could help protect and save or just bring final peace to those women who've vanished.

Still kneeling, he turns to Faustino.

—Vato, gimme your lighter.

Faustino hands him the lighter and then hobbles away.

—Don't take all night—he says over his shoulder.—You've got a card game to play.

Arturo nods. He flicks the lighter into life and looks at the candles. There are many different colors, a whole rainbow of colors. He doesn't suppose that it matters, so he chooses one nearest to him, one that has not been lit before, sitting in the piles of cigarettes and the notes and the little bundles of dollars, and he lights it.

—Bring her peace—he whispers.—Wherever she is.

"And one day, after five years of smoke, dust, and blindness, that cloud lifted, and two empires lay in the dust. No monarchy, no armies, only the enormity of the usurpation in ruins, and on that horrible rubble, one man standing: Benito Juárez, and next to him, Liberty.

"And do you know what Juárez did with that liberty? He could have shown mercy, he could have shown that his liberty was greater than the dictator he had deposed: Maximilian of Habsburg. Let the violator of Liberty be saved by Liberty.

"But what did Juárez do? Did he show Mercy to Maximilian? No. Instead, he had the deposed emperor executed; and so he chose to remain true to Death. In this way, the cycle of Death continued."

ON THE COUCH

As they drive down Rancho Anapra, Arturo looks at Faustino, steadily, wondering. He is wondering what has happened to his friend. He is wondering about many things, that all seem to have erupted this one evening, from nowhere, as if a wild devil has sprung into his sleepy life, determined to disrupt and destroy everything. He is afraid, and he knows it. He still cannot understand why Faustino has joined a gang, though he can guess easily enough. There are lots of reasons why; they'd seen enough guys they knew get involved with M-33, or whoever was ruling the turf around Anapra, to know that it was one way out of poverty, one quick way. But Faustino? It's just too much for Arturo, just too much to understand.

It is Friday evening, cars come and go, groups of people walk here and there in twos and threes. Normal people doing normal things, Arturo thinks, and here am I, with my friend Faustino. My old friend and nothing is wrong, really, and—

Arturo voices one of the things he is wondering, one of the simpler things.

—¿You still got that gun?

Faustino laughs.

He pulls over to the side of the road, stops the car. They haven't even left the colonia, but here, at the far end of Rancho Anapra, where the road rises for a short way before dropping down the hill into the pits of Juárez, is somewhere they both know well.

A strip of purple neon stolen from god-knows-what and god-knows-where illuminates the name above the door: El Diván. A single-story hut of concrete blocks, a few unoccupied chairs and a maltreated fake leather sofa, or couch, on the stoop. Already a raucous din is pouring from inside.

—I don't know about you—Faustino says—but I could do with a drink.

—You said we had to get to the game.

—Yeah. We do. But nothing's gonna be happening yet, anyway. No big money. And I need a drink.

He opens his door and puts his good foot out onto the ground, then turns and waits for Arturo.

—Mierda, so do I—says Arturo, and they head for the bar.

—¿When did you even learn to drive?—Arturo asks.

—A couple of Los Libertadores showed me.

—¿You pass some kind of test?

Faustino laughs again.

He pulls up his sleeve, briefly and flashes the two Ls inked on his arm.

—That's my license, vato. Any cop stops me, I show him that.

—¿And what if he isn't being paid off by the Azteca?

—Well, they can't take my license away. ¿Right?

No, thinks Arturo, but someone might take your arm away, just for having that tattoo. Faustino seems to know this too. He rolls his sleeve back down before they push their way through the doors and into the bar, because this is M-33 territory.

El Diván is about half full. People spending what little they've earned in the week. It's mostly men, a few women. A kid or two hanging around. There's a game of calavera under way at the usual table in the corner. Any other Friday night and Arturo would already be sitting there. Any Friday night a year ago and Faustino would have been sitting there too.

Carlos sees them straight away. He's barreling through the tables with a tray of beers and a bottle of tequila.

—¡Hey, muchachos! ¿Arturo, you playing tonight? ¡Faustino! ¿Where you been? Haven't seen you in forever. And this one wouldn't tell me where you'd got to.

He nods at Arturo, who shrugs.

—Don't ask me, Carlos. Ask him.

Carlos delivers the drinks to a table nearby, all locals that Arturo and Faustino know well enough.

—¿So?—Carlos asks.—¿What can I get you?

Faustino looks toward the bar.

—¿Isn't Siggy here?—he asks.

Carlos rolls his eyes.

—Sure. He's here. "El Alemán" is just in one of his moods . . . You know how he gets. I'll go find him. He might cheer up if he knows you're here. ¿You want a drink or what? ¿Beer, tequila? We got some pulque on the go, and Siggy got hold of a barrel of turbo, if you want something even stronger. But you don't wanna go there.

You wanna drink something that prisoners make and smuggle *out* of jail, you might as well be dead.

He can't stop chuckling, waving his hands in front of their faces, same Carlos as ever.

—Two beers—Arturo says.

Carlos rolls away, back toward the bar, where he sticks his head into the back room, shouting.

—¡Hey, Siggy! Get out here. ¡Arturo and Faustino are here! ¡They wanna see you!

Life heaves all around Arturo and Faustino as they find an empty table, and wait for their beers, nodding at people they know.

—¿Why do they call him that?—Arturo asks.—I never knew.

—¿Siggy, you mean? ¿El Alemán—the German? I guess because he's from Germany, cabrón.

—His Spanish is really good. He doesn't sound foreign.

—Carlos once told me he came to Mexico when he was still in his twenties or something. Dropped out of some fancy school in California when he was still a kid.

—¿And he ended up here? Dumb luck.

—He ended up with Carlos. And then they ended up here. There's a difference.

—¿What difference?

Faustino doesn't answer for a moment, and when he does, it's almost too quiet for Arturo to hear, but he thinks his friend has used the word *love*.

Before Arturo can ask, Siggy is wandering over. He looks as haggard as always, possibly hung over, his shoulders bent toward the floor. From somewhere he musters some energy, pulling his little round glasses down from his head and straightening them on his nose as he comes.

—¡Hola! ¡My friends!

They slap hands.

—¡Faustino! ¿Where you been?

—It's a long story.

Siggy nods.

—¿Aren't they all? ¿Arturo, you not playing tonight?

Arturo glances at the calavera game, the kind of game he'd usually play, a game for a few pesos at most. Then he looks away. He shakes his head.

There's a silence that no one fills, until Carlos wanders over with two bottles. Siggy puts his arm around Carlos's shoulder and whispers a word in his ear. Arturo lip-reads the word *sorry*, but then he's thinking about that narco with the tattooed face mouthing some word at him. ¿Was that only this afternoon? My God, thinks Arturo. That's not possible.

Siggy is speaking again.

—¿You guys in some kind of trouble?

—No, we're fine—says Faustino quickly, and then Arturo adds, just as quickly—Yeah. We are.

Carlos and Siggy look at each other, then Carlos sees people waiting at the bar, and heads away.

—Siggy, do not bend their heads with your nonsense—he says as he goes. ¿Right? ¡This time I mean it!

Siggy mocks looking hurt, then pulls up a chair and sits.

—Whole world's in trouble. ¿Right? The whole world's in trouble. But we don't care about that. ¿What's your part of it?

The friends do not answer. Arturo because he does not want to speak for Faustino, Faustino because he does not want to speak.

—I have learned one thing in my fifty years on this planet—Siggy says, very calmly, very quietly.

Faustino stares at the table.

Arturo waits for Siggy to go on.

—Life, as we find it, is too hard for us.

Faustino seems to be getting riled up again, and shakes his head angrily, but El Alemán ignores him.

—I may have said that before.

—About a million times—Faustino says, standing.—I need to take a piss.

He goes off and out through the back door, into the cool night of the sierra.

Siggy watches him go.

—¿What's eating him, Arturo?

Arturo shakes his head.

—I . . . can't tell you. I shouldn't tell you. Listen, Siggy . . . ¿What do you know about Santa Muerte?

—¿Is that it? ¿Faustino has become a muertista?

—No—says Arturo.—I mean, yes, he has, but that's not the problem. ¿Is it dangerous?

—¿Dangerous?—Siggy says.—No, not dangerous. In fact, as religious matters go, I would say it's pretty harmless.

—Faustino thinks it's powerful.

—Oh, religions have power. For sure.

—I thought you think religion is stupid.

—I do. All religion is patently infantile. But that doesn't mean it doesn't have power. Religions are given power by the people who believe in them. Personally, I believe that religion is the obsessive handwashing of a group of people who would otherwise be insane.

He points a finger toward the ceiling, and Arturo looks desperately for Carlos; for Siggy is about to embark on one of his rambles, and there is no one to save him. He sees Carlos behind the bar, too busy with customers to notice, and Siggy is just getting going.

—I admit that that in itself is not a bad thing; it is perhaps the one true benefit of religion. Religion is a collective delusion, a collective madness that ironically *prevents* madness for the individual, and I have to concede that's of benefit to all of us, even those of us outside of the group, for whom the religion has no power. ¿But within the group? ¡O God! ¡There is power, yes! And this Santa Muerte . . . she is something else. I would guess that very soon, as many Mexicans will pray to her as to the Virgin. So she has power. And the narcos pray to her, and the army, and the police, and the politicians and the prostitutes, and the prison guards and the prisoners, and the poor. The Church is scared of her, you know. ¡They have tried to ban her! You heard what the Pope said. ¿But do people care? No. They do what they have always done, they worship who they want to worship, and anything that the Catholic Church cannot control must be very powerful indeed. ¿But dangerous? No, I don't think so. What I think is dangerous is what is tattooed on our friend's other arm.

Arturo has only been half listening, but this gets his attention.
—¿You saw?

—A glimpse. And I don't know which gang he has joined, and I don't want to know. And it doesn't matter. Whichever one it is, *that's* what's dangerous.

Arturo lets out a long, slow breath. He knows this already. He thinks, hesitating, for a second, knowing that Faustino will be back any moment.

—¿Siggy, you remember Eva? She's had a baby, with Faustino. He's paid some coyotes to get her across to El Norte. Tonight.

Now Siggy looks worried.

—¿She's taking the baby with her?

Arturo nods.—¿You think it's dangerous?—he asks.

—So many people want to go to America. To escape the poverty, the violence. But maybe you're asking the wrong person. I was the one who came the other way.

Arturo thinks about that for a moment.—They're going to Los Angeles. ¿Isn't that where you're from?

Siggy holds Arturo's gaze for a moment, then he seems to disappear somewhere. His eyes look into the past, the distant past of things seen and done a very long time ago. He doesn't speak, and Arturo stares around the bar, awkwardly. He knows how Siggy gets sometimes, everyone does. The darkness in his eyes, bottomless. But it's something else to have it happen to you, and because of something you said.

—Let me tell you something—Siggy whispers, rubbing the corners of his eyes with thumb and forefinger up under his glasses.

Arturo nods.

—Forgive me—Siggy adds—but it's about myself.

72

—That's okay—says Arturo. He even finds a smile. He could listen to Siggy all day, though it's hard to hear what he's saying, he speaks so quietly.

—No one here knows who I am—he says, but he gets no further because Carlos is wandering over, chiding at the top of his voice.

—Siggy, I told you not to—he's saying, but then realizes his friend is barely speaking at all, never mind bending Arturo's ear. He puts his hand on Siggy's shoulder.

—¿You okay?—he asks.

Siggy grasps Carlos's hand and holds it firmly. He whispers more.

—Only my good friend Carlos knows who I am. Only Carlos. ¿Right, my friend?

Carlos smiles but Arturo can see it's forced. Carlos pats his friend's shoulder, gently.

—Siggy—he says—we need some more beer. Bring a couple of crates from out back, muchacho. I think Arturo's heard enough today. ¿Right?

Siggy nods his head, as if he's very, very tired. He stands. He looks old, older than fifty. His face is lined and his hair straggly and gray; the long stubble on his chin is white. He blinks, smiles at Carlos, then he sees Faustino coming back over to join them, and he leans down so that only Arturo can hear, before whispering— I hope Faustino chose his coyotes well.

Then Faustino is there, and Siggy smiles and slaps him on the back.

—I gotta get to work. Good to see you.

Faustino nods, then downs his beer in one go.

—And we gotta get to work too—he says, looking at Arturo—Leave your beer, vato. Or drink up. It's time to go.

Carlos watches them leave, Arturo following his friend into the start of the night, El Alemán's words ringing in his head.

I hope Faustino chose his coyotes well.

:-PorMiMexico22 wrote:

Monday afternoon, 160,000 liters of meth precursors found in 800 200-liter drums in warehouse in Comitán, Chiapas, near southern border. The shelves contained election propaganda for the recently elected mayor. *"When the system's corrupt, what can you do but run?"*

:-beelucky151 wrote:

I have sympathy. I do. But it's just how things are, right? What are you gonna do?

:-PorMiMexico22 wrote:

Just because it's how things are doesn't mean we shouldn't try to do something about it. That it can't change. No? Perhaps this is the modern version of Faust; that we sit around writing stuff or wringing our hands saying, yes, yes, but what can *we* do about it?

:-beelucky151 is typing:

You think you know everything? You ever even been there? Anyway, life's cheaper down there, right? So it doesn't matter if they don't earn as much as . . .

CIUDAD JUÁREZ

In front of the car in which Arturo and Faustino journey through the night, down the long, dark hill, Juárez waits, haunting their futures, and ours.

Juárez: the ultimate goal, our final destination; the inevitable end to the path we are taking, the inescapable culmination of the world we are making. We might look away, but whether we look away or not, it's there. It lies at the bottom of the road down from the sierra, a hot beast in a cold world of night, from which streetlights can be seen, and where a fire rages over near the border and now, across in some colonia or other, muzzle flashes of gunfire pierce the darkness. Juárez is what occurs when greed makes money by passing things across the border dividing poverty and wealth. Things like cars, like electronics, like machines. Things like drugs, things like people.

Arturo feels his gut squirm. All he has: in his right pocket, seventy dollars, in his left, his Catrina knife. That's all. That's not quite all.

Three lampposts in a row painted pink, bearing fading black crosses: symbol of the missing women. Arturo watches Faustino's face as they pass under the lights, the orange glow that grows steadily then vanishes quickly as each lamp goes by. He cannot make out his friend's face clearly, in this soft slow strobe, and he is struck by a horrible feeling: that he is sitting next to a stranger.

¿Why did you leave me? he thinks, then it seems that maybe he said it out loud, for Faustino turns to look at him. That anger is still there, challenging Arturo, daring him to say the wrong thing, to do the wrong thing, whatever that might be.

Faustino fishes behind his back as he drives, and wriggles the gun out of his pants, sets it on the dashboard.

—¿What are you doing?—Arturo asks.

—¿See that?—Faustino says.—I want to explain something to you. So answer me a question: ¿Where did I get that from?

Arturo doesn't want to answer the question. He wants an answer to his own. *¿Why did Faustino just go? ¿Why didn't he say what he was doing, why didn't he keep in touch?* Because he just went, leaving Arturo with . . .

—¿Where did the gun come from?—Faustino says, sounding edgy.

—I don't know—says Arturo.—¿The gang? I guess someone in Los Libertadores gave it to you. Yeah, you told me that.

—Yeah. ¿But where did they get it from?

—No idea, vato—says Arturo.

—It came from El Norte.

—Yeah. Most guns do. ¿Right?

—Yeah. ¿Except you know how this one got here?

Arturo sighs. He doesn't like the game that Faustino is playing because he doesn't know the rules. He also doesn't like the way Faustino has been changing his mind about things all night. But he makes a guess at Faustino's question.

—Some narco gave money to a straw buyer in Texas or New Mexico and he went to a gun dealer and then either smuggled the gun over the border himself or the narco went to get it.

—Very good—says Faustino and Arturo wants to hit him, but Faustino doesn't notice or doesn't care.

—But this is where it gets weird—he says.—¿You know who the straw buyer was really working for?

—I don't—mutters Arturo.

—The ATF. Alcohol, Tobacco, and Fireams. The Americans. ¿And you know what's even weirder? The money that the narco gave to the straw so he could buy guns that would be brought over here for the cartel to use—that came from the CIA.

—¿What? ¿They stole CIA money?

—You're not paying attention. The CIA *gave* the cartel the money to buy the guns.

—No way, cabrón. That's messed up. ¿Why would they do that?

—¿Why? They did it to arm the Sinaloa cartel to the teeth so they could wipe out the CDJ. They gave the Sinaloans a quarter of a million dollars to buy guns and then let them walk those guns over here to use against the cartel here. That's why.

Arturo is shaking his head.

—¿When was this?—he asks.

—Years back; the turf wars were bad then, when we were kids. When the women were going missing.

Arturo ignores that last remark.

—¿And who told you all this? ¿You believe it?

—El Carnero himself told me. Told me how the Sinaloans moved into Juárez, right into CDJ territory. They were fighting for control of the bridge, the drug route to El Norte. Things are different now, now it's just total anarchy. But the guns are still here, and mine is one of them.

Arturo doesn't really understand, let alone believe what he's hearing.

—¿El Carnero told you this? ¿Why?

—He told me for the same reason I'm telling you, pendejo.

Faustino starts shouting. From nowhere, for some reason, that anger has welled up again and bursts out.

—¡I'm telling you because you are a dumb little kid! ¡I'm telling you because nothing in Juárez is what you think it is! That's what El Carnero told me: do not trust anything, not even what your own eyes show you. Everything is chingada, and the only way you stay alive is by being faster and smarter than everyone else. ¿Got it?

Arturo says nothing.

—¿You got it?—Faustino shouts and then Arturo snaps.

—Yeah. I got it. Faster and smarter than everyone else. Just like you. ¿Right?

Faustino curses. He presses his bad foot to the gas pedal and they speed into the belly of the city. It swallows them.

So, we are all god-killers. We kill the gods that came before us and we put up new gods in their place. We erect a new totem to be worshipped, just as, in some unknown distant past, we erected the first totem, after we committed the first murder, the primal killing.

In that distant past, we killed what came before us, and then, erecting a totem in its name, we made that murder taboo, we made murder itself taboo.

We handed the right to kill to that thing we call civilization. Civilization does our killing for us, and we can wash our hands of it. This is the management of death.

But the blood will not wash off. We live with the blood of that first killing on our hands, eternally.

LA CIVILIZACIÓN Y SUS DESCONTENTOS

They are on the outskirts of the city now, crossing thresholds. Ahead lie totems: at a Pemex station the hill levels out and they pass half-built homes from which weak lights shine. The road climbs for a while, until, passing an ugly, modern church, it drops down more steeply to the city itself. Here, a tall yellow monument dominates the traffic circle, and Arturo knows they are beside the river, just to their left, though here its banks are made of concrete, the river funneled through the city to suppress the force of water and the attempted crossings of immigrants. A fence broken in places lines the Mexican side; on the far bank there's a much higher fence topped with razor wire. Beyond it is America, the unknown land.

They move on.

Faustino guides the car around streets that he seems to know well, streets that Arturo has never seen before.

They swing this way and that, making slow turns at lights, and Arturo sees that Friday night in the city is well underway. Sirens wail. Neon burns on all sides, bodies come and go, people standing on street corners, heading out of bars, heading into bars. Without exception, they are all seeking something; few know what it is they seek.

Faustino makes a couple more turns and they leave the hubbub behind. These are narrower, darker streets.

—This is Chaveña—Faustino says quietly.

A few buildings have two stories, most have only one. All have bars across every window, some have razor wire on their fences and gates, at the edges of roofs.

At a crossroads, Faustino pulls the car onto a vacant piece of ground, and stops the engine.

—Calle Libertad—he says.—I can't go any closer, in case someone sees me.

Arturo stares out at the street, half lit by orange streetlights. He doesn't like the half he sees.

—Go up this way—Faustino is saying.—Turn left on Insurgentes. There's a big junction, with a fountain in the middle. Take the second street on your right. Halfway down on the left, you'll see the bar. It's called El Alacrán.

Arturo does not move, does not speak. He stares out through the windshield at the near-deserted street. He's having trouble understanding that Faustino wants him to leave, go out into the night, walk into a rough bar in a rough part of the city, and play cards to save his life. But that is exactly what Faustino seems to expect him to do.

—The big money starts to go down soon—Faustino is saying.— But you don't have big money. So you need to catch the tail end of a game where they're still playing for fives and tens.

—I know how to make money—Arturo says.

—¿So what's the problem?

Faustino seems to think he's asking Arturo to go buy some groceries for him.

—Listen—says Faustino.—I'll wait here. No matter how long it takes. I'll wait here. ¿You see that place, right opposite? That's my place. I mean, it belongs to El Carnero but he's been letting Eva and me stay there since her mother chucked us out. When you have the money, come back here and I'll get you out. ¿Right?

When I have the money, thinks Arturo. ¿When? ¿Not if?

He looks across the dimly lit street to the building that Faustino calls *his place*. It's a one-story building of cinder block, painted green in parts. There's a battered red door with bars over it, with the number 965 in peeling white paint.

—Here—Faustino says.—Take this, buy a beer with it. Don't use the dollars for that.

He puts a small wad of pesos in Arturo's hand.

—That's half of what I've got left in the world right now—Faustino says.—Be careful with it.

Arturo finds that he is nodding his head. He finds that he is saying okay to Faustino. He finds he is slipping the pesos into the pocket of his shirt. He even finds that he has one hand on the catch that opens the car door, though he does not remember putting it there.

—Just one thing—Arturo says.—Tell me this one thing, and then I will go.

Faustino appears to relax a little. Maybe just the sign that Arturo is going to go is enough to allow some of his anger to evaporate into the night.

—Sure. ¿What?

—Tell me why you left me.

Faustino shakes his head. He sighs, but he doesn't seem angry.

—¿Really?

—Really.

—Truth is, vato. I don't know. I mean, I know I'd had enough. Of having no money, of nothing to do, nothing to live for. And we wanted more, Eva and me. We both did. And things were okay till her mother chucked us out. Then the only thing I could do was . . .

He trails off, and Arturo knows he means how he joined the gang.

—But you could have told me—Arturo says.

—I could have . . .—Faustino says.—But something stopped me. I missed you. Yeah, I did. I missed you a lot. I had Eva, of course, but . . .

—¿So why didn't you come and find me? ¿Tell me what you were doing?

Faustino shrugs.

—I don't know. Like I said, something stopped me. I didn't want to get you into anything.

—¿Anything?—asks Arturo, almost left speechless by how dumb his friend is.—¿Anything like this, you mean?

He pops the door open.

—Wish me luck, pendejo.

He steps out of the car, and is about to shut the door when Faustino calls out.

—¡Hey, Arturo! The candles at Doña Maria's. ¿Which one did you light?

Arturo is confused.

—¿Which one? I don't know. The nearest one.

—No, I don't mean that. ¿What color did you light?

Arturo thinks for a second. He sees all the candles around Santa Muerte's feet, the ofrenda: the money, the cigarettes, the glasses of water. He sees the slips of paper; the prayers left to the impartial saint, a universal warrior.

He sees himself pulling the lighter from Faustino's hand, sees himself scratching a flame from it, and sees the color of the candle he chose to light.

—Black—he tells Faustino.—¿Why?

Faustino shakes his head, mutters under his breath.

—Maybe it's for the best—he says.—Good luck, Arturo.

—¿Why? ¿What does it mean?

—Get out of here, cabrón. Someone's coming. We shouldn't be seen together. Not here.

Arturo sees two young men walking on the other side of Libertad.

—¿What does it mean, Faustino? Tell me.

Faustino is getting mad.

—It means a bunch of stuff. Protection. Now get out of here. Go and be a god.

—¿Protection? That's good. ¿Right?

Faustino leans across and grabs the door handle, slamming it, shutting himself in. He waves Arturo away.

The two men are getting nearer; they may not be anyone, but there is no way of telling.

So Arturo goes.

FIRST GAME

Arturo finds El Alacrán all too easily; it is a jumping wolf pit in an otherwise shadow-laden and empty street. Opposite is a shop that used to repair things, but it's derelict and half the sign has fallen off, making it impossible to know what those things were. A barber's stands next to that, and a lady's hairdresser. Every building is a squalid mixture of the half-built and semi-ruined, and yet life of a kind is here. Just an hour ago these places were still open for business; behind the bars of the barber's a light shines, showing someone cleaning up.

Down a side alley, Arturo hears a ruckus: the snarling and baying of men and hounds; a dog fight in full fray, but even that sound is almost drowned out by the noise from El Alacrán itself.

Arturo tries to ignore the misgivings in his head, in his heart, and knows he will not be able to play until the trembling in his fingers has subsided. He tells himself that another drink will fix that, and without allowing himself to think further walks up to the two men on the door, remembering what Faustino told him to say.

—I want to play. I have dollars.

The two men look at him. They are perhaps less than ten years older than him, but they are dark gods with guns and easy brutality, and he is just Arturo. They don't seem to care.

One of them spreads his fingertips out on Arturo's chest, barring his way.

—Show us.

Arturo pulls out the roll of dollars, hoping it looks more like hundreds than just seventy.

The man nods.

—Okay. ¿You packing?

Arturo shakes his head, even before he wonders whether they count a knife as *packing*. And even before he can correct himself, they stand aside and Arturo finds he has walked inside, realizing that he must look just as puny as he actually is.

It is dark. There are harsh lights on the walls that seem to do a better job of blinding than illuminating the room. Music is pumping from speakers fixed to the ceiling; angry and proud narcocorridas about the fantastic cop-killing exploits of some gang hero. There's a long bar down the whole of one wall, on the end of which two girls are dancing, wearing only red bikinis and knee-high white boots. They pay more attention to each other than to the gaggle of men watching them. The place is packed, but as his eyes adjust, Arturo sees a bunch of tables at the far end of the place, and knows that calavera is being played there.

He tries to be cool, pushing and squeezing past hot bodies on his way to the bar, where he buys a beer with some of the pesos Faustino gave him.

—I wanna play—he tells the barman.

The barman just points at the tables.

—Go find an empty chair—he says.—And be lucky.

The room is full of narcos. As Arturo makes his way to the calavera tables, he sees men with the same tattoo that Faustino has,
the two long Ls—Los Libertadores. This is their patch, they are
home, it is Friday night. They appear relaxed; there is laughter and
shouting, but it's good-natured shouting. It's not really much different from El Diván.

That's what Arturo tells himself as he gets to the tables. There
are four of them. Three of them are packed, with six or seven guys
seated around each one, and more standing, looking on, so Arturo
goes to the fourth table, where there are only four men playing.
There are two empty chairs.

The men look up as Arturo stands over them. One of them is
an oldish guy, stocky and bald. His sleeves are rolled up, there are
no tattoos, which makes Arturo relax a little. The three younger
guys meanwhile stare at Arturo, and with a touch of menace, but
he cannot help that now. One of them is clearly green, new to the
game: a pendejo just waiting to get burned; the second is a fat guy
with a fat mustache and short, cropped hair that doesn't entirely
hide a thick scar across his skull. The third wears his thinning hair
oiled back flat. His eyes don't stop roving. It's obvious he's very nervous and trying to hide it by drinking frequently.

The fat guy stares at Arturo, not hiding his contempt.

—¿What do you want, kid?

—I want to play calavera, and yes, I have dollars.

The fat guy just stares back at Arturo, who acts as cool as he can, despite the eyes on him. There's a clumsy moment, as all four stare at him, just stare.

Arturo points at one of the empty seats.

The bald guy nods.

—Sure. If you can handle the stakes.

¿Can I handle the stakes? thinks Arturo, as he sits down.

It's a good question, he knows. It's a very good question, but he cannot back out now and there is only one way to find out.

The four men have just finished a hand. The sucker rakes the pile of dollars in, laughing at his good fortune.

Arturo sees what they're using as the calaverita: a small white stone that almost looks like the miniature skull it's supposed to be.

The stone sits in front of the older, bald guy, showing that he's running the bank, and doesn't seem fazed by a pile of his dollars heading into the pockets of the pendejo, at his right-hand side.

The bald man holds the stone out across the table toward Arturo.

—¿You want it?

Of course, Arturo knows, it's the custom when playing calavera to offer a newcomer to the table the chance to run the bank. He just had no idea they'd stick to such codes of conduct here.

Arturo shakes his head quickly, and the three younger men laugh. The bald guy puts the stone back down in front of him, smiling.

—Maybe later—he says, and Arturo doesn't care that he's smirking as he says it, because Arturo thinks, Yeah. You just keep thinking I'm some dumb pendejo. Keep thinking that and when I've won a stack of your dollars maybe I *will* take the bank. And then I'll rob all of you.

It's only then that Arturo notices something. The pack of cards. It looks damn fat. It looks way too fat to be a single deck, and Arturo realizes with a sinking heart that they're using two decks. Two decks. One of the reasons Arturo is so good at calavera is that he remembers the cards that have been played. That means that at any moment he has a slightly better chance of gambling well than the pendejos he plays with, the suckers who think it's all down to luck. It evens up the slight advantage that the banker has by dealing his cards last, by knowing what's been played before *he* makes *his* move. Arturo has only played with two decks once before. He didn't like it.

The bald man offers the first bank.

—Let's go easy on the kid—he says.—Twenty dollars.

The fat guy, who's sitting to his left, nods and slides his twenty across the table. So does the guy with the nervous eyes.

Then it's Arturo; he nods and slides two tens out; finally the sucker shows he wants in too, and puts his money on the table.

The music is thumping as two cards come down to each of them and Arturo thinks, Please, please, please, and then he knows it's going to be a good night, because he's been dealt a nine, straight off.

—Calavera—he says calmly, just loud enough to be heard over the din. He flips his cards over.

The three young guys laugh and shove their cards into the center. The bald guy deals himself his banker's hand and turns them: an eight.

—Close—he says.—You're a lucky kid. ¿Am I right?

Arturo shrugs and pulls the hundred dollars over the table toward him.

—Fifty dollars—announces the bald man, and again everyone goes in. It's way more than Arturo wants to play at the moment, before he's won some capital to work with. But he has no choice. He could sit the round out, of course, but then they'd know how little he brought with him in the first place, and then they'd know they could wipe him out fast.

Luck is on Arturo's side. He holds a four with his first two cards and when he takes the option of a third he makes an eight, which wins. Including the seventy he showed up with, he now has in his hands three hundred and fifty dollars.

They play another hand, and another, and after the fifth the nervous guy takes over the bank. Arturo has lost twice, won big once more. He holds just under five hundred dollars. It is more money than he has ever held in his life, way more money than he has ever even seen in his life. He's winning. And yet, it is less than halfway toward what he needs. What *Faustino* needs.

He knows he must hold his nerve. So far, he's been coping with the two decks, an advantage that will only really kick in when enough hands have gone down. If he makes it that far, he'll really have them where he wants them.

He must hold his nerve, but halfway through the third of these hands he'd gotten scared. He sat on his five, when he should have drawn, but then five is the turning point in the game; the whole skill of calavera, the whole reason his memory of which cards have been played gives him an edge, is down to what you do on the five. He got scared, he sat, and he lost. Then he decided that he needed to forget they were playing with dollars. Midway through the next deal he decided to tell himself they were playing with pesos. He tries to imagine that the twenty-dollar notes in front of him are hundred-peso notes instead. On the hundred-peso note, Arturo knows, is the image of Nezahualcoyotl, philosopher and warrior king. He stares at the dead American president in front of him. His name reads "Jackson." Arturo has no idea who he is, and tries hard to turn him into the ancient ruler of Tetzcoco instead.

They play on, with the pendejo now holding the bank. Arturo's strategy seems to be working. He sips at the bottle of beer, making sure not to slug it down, telling himself not to drink so fast he loses his edge, not to drink so little they know he's trying to avoid paying for another.

The pendejo is a terrible banker, makes some stupid decisions, and gets himself cleaned out, something everyone could see coming. Arturo watches it happen with a sick feeling in his stomach, and delight too. It occurs so easily, so quickly. He's seen it many times, the recklessness, the desperation, the hasty gamble on a hunch. Frustration making an idiot of someone. The pendejo started throwing down crazy amounts for the bank, lost three times and was cleaned out.

Arturo lost a couple of times too, but despite the fact that working with two decks is frying his brain, he now sits on seven hundred and ten dollars. It's going well. All he needs to do is to keep his cool, not make any rash bets, and edge his total up to the thousand. And the second he has a thousand, he's walking. Unlike the pendejo, he's not stupid, he doesn't take risks, and that's why he wins at calavera.

Then, the world shakes and everything falls apart. There's been a crowd of people watching them play, just like at the other tables. Arturo hasn't looked at them once, he's just been concentrating on his game, and people have come and gone, but then, without warning and without knowing why, he looks up and sees a face staring at him.

The face has tattoos covering it. They are the double L, interlocked across from his left cheek to his right, across his nose. It's the narco who took Gabriel earlier today, whose fingertip Arturo can still feel pressing into his forehead, and he's standing right behind the bald guy.

He holds Arturo's gaze for a moment, expressionless. There's a break in the music, silence fills the room. Arturo doesn't even hear the chatter that's going on all around him. He just stares at the narco, unable to look away. The bald guy is waiting for Arturo to play, and turns to see who he's looking at.

—¡Hey!—he says, his face brightening.—¡Raúl!

They clasp their arms together, wrapping their forearms around each other and holding hands briefly. They know each other well, it's clear.

And then the narco, Raúl, says—¡Hey, Eduardo! ¿How's it going? ¿Is El Carnero winning?

Arturo freezes, hoping he misheard, hoping he didn't really hear what he just did.

El Carnero. Raúl called him El Carnero. O God. O Jesus fucking God.

El Carnero is asking Raúl something.

—¿You finished?—he says, and Raúl nods, grinning, and

96

Arturo sees the traces of blood at his wrists, fresh blood, as the music comes back on, raging and drilling music that wants to be let loose on the world and do harm.

The bald guy, El Carnero, turns to the game again.

—¿You in?—he shouts across to Arturo, who nods, hardly able to breathe, let alone think. He is playing calavera with the man who will kill Faustino unless he can take a thousand dollars off him by the end of the night.

Standing right behind him is the narco who abducted Gabriel from Anapra that morning.

Arturo plays, but he cannot think straight. He drinks quickly, he cannot keep track of the two decks anymore. And he begins to lose.

Most Holy Death
The favors that you grant me
Will make me overcome any troubles that come my way
And help me see that nothing is impossible.
Not treacherous obstacles, not one enemy,
Nor let one person harm me.
Let only friends come into my path,
And let my business flourish,
And let everything I do flourish.
Fill my house with riches,
And protect those riches with your power.
Most Holy Death,
In your name, I beseech you,
Bring me from all harm.

CALAVERA

The bar roils. All across the room, unbridled emotions beat their drum, louder than the modern electric, synthetic drums of the narco-corridas. The drums that beat underneath are older; immeasurably ancient and much more powerful. The girls on the bar move their bodies. Men watch them. Other men roar and tip tequila or beer down their throats and, slapping each other on the back, they laugh. In one corner, a dispute between two men threatens to erupt and one grabs the other by the neck of his shirt. The barman nods to the thugs on the door who keep an eye on it but do not move, and in the far corner, at the card tables, Arturo plays cards for Faustino's life.

Here, the world bends around a small stone that represents a bone. The calaverita resides once more at the fingertips of El Carnero. It is the skull bone of history; it comes from the skeleton of a long and as yet unended story about violence and death, where, atop this skeleton, sits the calavera itself: the skull after which the card game is named. We all have a deep desire, a deep *need*, to ignore what is happening here. We do so in order that we can go on, day after day, but this is *our* future we are so very keen not to look at, and it rolls toward us, regardless of whether we choose to look away.

At least, here, tonight in Chaveña, in El Alacrán, the truth of the world is closer to the surface, easier to see. Death is the totem that the bar dances to, and nothing is taboo.

It is at this moment, as the fathers and mothers of Mexico decompose in long-forgotten and frequently unmarked graves, that El Carnero puts down a bank of a hundred dollars.

—¿Who's in?

There are just the four of them left. The pendejo is long gone, away to whatever it is awaiting him, leaving El Carnero, the fat man with the fat scar, the nervous guy, and Arturo.

Arturo hesitates.

He looks up and sees that Raúl is talking to El Carnero. He cannot hear what's being said over the noise of the bar, but he sees the narco look at him from time to time, and knows he is being spoken of.

Arturo looks down at the money in his fist, held just under the edge of the table. Then he goes in, putting down two fifty-dollar notes, distracted, disarmed.

The cards come down.

He gets a four. He takes another card and gets a ten. The hundred dollars goes with the rest to El Carnero's pile.

Another bank of a hundred.

—¿Who's in?

This time he sits on a six and loses to the nervous guy's natural calavera.

Five of his twenties disappear across the table.

He knows the cards have left him. It happens this way and when it happens, it's time to stop and walk away. In his hands he holds three hundred and forty dollars. He should leave now and take what he has to Faustino. Maybe it's enough. Maybe somehow they can find the rest before tomorrow night. He should walk away, but just moments ago he had so much more. He wants it back.

—¿Who's in?

Arturo sees that El Carnero has put down another bank of a hundred.

He nods and slides five more twenties into the center of the table.

The cards come down, and Arturo thinks, Please, please, please, and—

—¡Calavera! yells the nervous guy, who's looking less nervous by the minute. A second natural in a row and Arturo knows for sure that that is where the cards have gone, that is where the luck has gone, and that he should walk away.

—¿Who's in?—asks El Carnero, and Arturo nods and he's waiting for his cards to come down when he becomes aware that everyone is looking at him, staring, waiting. The guy with the scar on his right nudges him.

It takes him a moment to realize why. Arturo has already slid his hundred into the middle of the table, but then he sees that the bank is not one hundred. It's two. They're trying to wipe him out. He has just two hundred and forty dollars left. He slides the two hundred across the table and after him the cholo tosses his money onto the pile with a sneer on his face and then, just for a moment, Arturo shuts his eyes.

Calavera, the skull. The symbol of all our vanity. We dress and we preen and we strive and we love and we fight and we cry and we hurt and we love again and we undress and dress again and we are proud and afraid and jealous, we are oh so jealous and more than that we are afraid, afraid, we are terrified and yet something keeps us going, something that keeps us moving in spite of everything, but that something . . . ? That something is vanity itself.

For the skull does not care. The skull is what we all are, what we all will be and it is our equal and it makes us all equal, whether we are emperors or dogs in the gutter. The cards come down: a nine and a six and so, once more, Arturo holds a five.

Five is the turning point; the moment of truth, five is the only real test in calavera; this is the skill: to decide, when dealt a five, whether to draw another card, or not. The spent cards dance past Arturo's mind and they are laughing and jeering, taunting him and they will not be quiet and in desperation, he takes a card.

He draws five, and loses.

The fat guy has broken his losing streak with an eight, and laughs at the nervous guy, whose nerves suddenly return. El Carnero looks calmly across at Arturo and Arturo lifts his head and sees the man who will have Faustino killed, and the man who he will probably get to do it, staring at him.

Raúl lifts his hand and makes it into a gun. He pulls back his thumb as a hammer and then drops it, mouthing something as he does, mouthing the same thing he did earlier, in the street in Anapra.

Now Arturo knows what it is.

—Estás muerto.

That's what he said, that's what he's whispering now as he blows imaginary smoke off the tip of his forefinger, like a little kid.

—Estás muerto.

Arturo has only forty dollars left. He's through. He doesn't look at them as he speaks.

—I'm out—he says.

Without waiting for anyone to say anything, he gets up and walks away from the table, thirty dollars poorer than when he sat down two hours ago, and two hours closer to Faustino's death.

He pushes through the sweating heave of the bodies, all dancing, all dancing, all dancing closer to the moment at which their vanity is finally displayed to them, and half stumbles out into the street.

He does not know what to do.

He cannot go back to Faustino. He cannot tell him he had over seven hundred dollars in his hand, and blew it. He cannot tell him he blew it because he panicked when he realized he'd sat down with El Carnero.

Instead, he crosses the street and sits on the step of the barber's, which is now in total darkness, uncaring that the creatures at the door are looking at him from time to time.

They soon get bored.

Arturo does not know what to do, and yet, there *is* something.

No one knows where she came from, not really. Some say she came from Europe, and others say she came from South America. Some say she came from Mexico all along, though it wasn't called Mexico then. But everyone agrees on one thing: she does not discriminate. She opens her arms to all; she welcomes everyone in and will answer anyone who calls for her aid. Arturo knew of her before tonight. He knew her by sight. He saw, like everyone else, how there are more candles in the market than before, candles shaped like her. And figures, small ones and large ones, for sale on those same market stalls. He has seen those figures more often than before in the parades on Días de los Muertos; along with all the dark and sexy Catrinas and eternally laughing skeletons, along with all the little sugar skulls to be eaten, she's been there, waiting.

And tonight, he got down on his knees, and he prayed to her.

He knows his mother is dead. He does not know how, or who did it, or where her body ended up; she was simply one of the missing; that's all. Tonight, Arturo prayed to Santa Muerte to somehow bring her soul some peace, and he lit a candle, a black candle that Faustino told him means *protection*, so maybe that's good.

But there was something else, something that Faustino did not know about. As he knelt before the shrine, it seemed to Arturo crazy that people who desperately need money would leave money behind on the Skinny Girl's altar. He didn't care much about the pesos, but there were dollars there too. Dollars. Dollars, which, as Faustino called *Don't be long* over his shoulder, Arturo slipped into his shoe.

It seemed to him that Santa Muerte was telling him to take the money, that she knew he would need it tonight, not just a pathetic seventy dollars, so he quickly picked up the two largest rolls of green American money and slipped them inside his shoe.

He'd stood, looked Faustino in the eye, wished Doña Maria a good evening and thanked her for letting them use the shrine, and he had told himself that Santa Muerte must have wanted him to have the money.

He slides the two rolls out of his shoe now, and unfurls them.

He counts eighty-three dollars. He has forty left of what he came with. One hundred and twenty-three. Enough for one hand, maybe two, if they're going easy on the bank, and *yes*, Santa Muerte *wanted* him to have it.

That is one possibility, but there is another.

The other possibility is that he stole money from desperate people, who gave money to their dirty saint in their hour of need. That he stole money given to Santa Muerte. That he has tried to cheat death herself.

He stands, and walks back across the street.

SECOND GAME

He's thinking of his mother as he walks back toward the bar. Why she should invade his thoughts now is not clear to him, he only finds images of her in his vision; her hair, her smile. Her arms. Her warm arms.

He was eleven years old. He went to school one morning, one morning during that brief time when he and Faustino went to school. Meanwhile she went to work in the maquiladora, as usual, where she should have spent the day in a factory assembling a small part of a television set that would be sold north of the border and bear the words *Made in America*.

She never made it to work. The company bus broke down, a mile from the plant. It happened all the time, so no one complained, they just got out, and began to walk, and trot, because time was moving. While others ran, Arturo's mother was feeling ill, and could not, and because she was three minutes late reporting for her shift, they turned her away. The last time she was seen was by some of her fellow workers, setting off to make the long walk home.

She never made it, while the TVs she should have made were loaded into boxcars to join others rumbling on the Union Pacific line, like they still rumble now, every night, right past Arturo's shack. He rarely thinks about his mother. Not now, not these days. She's gone and he knows she's not coming back, just one of the disappeared women of Juárez, one of the thousands.

He thinks about what Faustino said: that wild story about American money financing the Sinaloa cartel against the CDJ. That was the time when the missing was at its worst. Girls, young women just being fed into the horror machine of the drug wars and the murders, playthings of men too wrapped up in the narco life to know they were already dead, that what they did to those women would be done to them the next day, or the day after.

Arturo nods to the guys at the door, and enters.

It seems El Alacrán has not been waiting for him; things progress exactly as they did before. He goes to the bar and with more of Faustino's pesos buys another bottle of beer, and then he heads back to the game.

It's still just the three of them, while the other tables are packed. Arturo knows why now: most people are too scared to play calavera with the jefe of Los Libertadores.

Arturo remembers what Faustino told him; what El Carnero had told him. *Nothing is what it seems.* If he had remembered that, he might have thought twice about sitting down with the old, bald guy to play cards. He looks strong, he's not as old as all that, but he's stocky, maybe even a little overweight. He looks nothing like the boss of a pandilla, but then, Arturo thinks, maybe it's the best disguise for such a man. And by avoiding tattoos, he's been smart; whereas Raúl displays his affiliation to Los Libertadores right across his sinful face. For better, or worse.

El Carnero looks up as Arturo approaches, and Arturo decides to get the first word in.

—Needed another one of these—he says, waving the beer.— ¿Can I?

He indicates the empty seat.

El Carnero doesn't reply to that, so Arturo sits down. Instead he asks—¿Where you from, niño?

Arturo's heart quickens. He thinks just as quickly. It cannot be that El Carnero knows who he is. He cannot know that he is a friend of Faustino. And until tomorrow night, he cannot know that Faustino has stolen a thousand dollars from him. He briefly thinks about lying, but knows it is best to tell the truth where the truth cannot hurt you. There is less to remember that way, whereas if you lie, you have to remember every damn lie you told.

—Anapra—Arturo says, trying to sound like it's kind of a boring question.

—¿Anapra?

El Carnero turns to Raúl, who's sitting in one of the empty seats now, though he's not playing.

—You were in Anapra today. ¿Right?

Raúl nods, looks toward Arturo. He is an arm's length away. He could reach out now and snap Arturo's head off with one hand.

—Yeah—he says.—¿Maybe you saw me?

Arturo shrugs.

—I guess so. Maybe. Or maybe not. ¿You know?

Raúl laughs. Arturo doesn't like it.

—Smart kid—Raúl says, to El Carnero, and Arturo wonders what the look that passes between them might mean. Then Raúl points two fingers right at him.

—¿What do you do in Anapra, niño?

Arturo shrugs again, fighting the urge to get up and run, run hard.

—I work for some guy. Auto shop.

—¿Yeah?—says Raúl.—¿What's his name? I could do with my truck getting looked at. Maybe he can help me out. There's this noise under the hood.

El Carnero taps the table with the calaverita.

—Raúl, not now. We're playing cards. ¿Aren't we? ¿We're playing cards, right?

He addresses this to Arturo, and waits for an answer.

—Yeah. I'm in.

Raúl slides his chair back a bit and El Carnero holds the stone out to Arturo once more, who once more refuses.

—¿No?—El Carnero laughs, shaking his head.—Maybe later then.

Arturo tries not to give anything away. He wants to give nothing to this man, not even an emotion, not even a thought. As it stands he has given him, and the other calavera players, a total of thirty dollars. That's all. He intends to get them back, and many more with them, but it will all depend on the first hand.

Arturo expects the bank to be a hundred dollars, and it is. He pulls out a hundred from his shirt pocket like he's got five times

110

that amount on him, and drops it into the middle of the table, and he keeps his eyes open as his cards come down and he's praying to Santa Muerte, Please, please, please.

He sees that the Bony Lady is playing games with him. She could have given him calavera, just to show she's on his side, that the cards have returned, that things are going to be good.

Instead, she gives him a five, and he must decide. The five again, the turning point, the moment of truth. La hora de la hora. He lost on the five, got wiped out. He took a card when he should have sat.

¿Why a five on the first damn hand? he thinks, but he knows why. She's testing him. He stole from her, no—no, she wanted him to have it. But he cannot know which of those is true and, in the meantime, she's going to test his faith.

He's holding a queen and a five and that makes a count of five.

Take a card or sit? Arturo did not see the previous hands; there is no way of knowing what lies in the discarded pile.

He must guess. Or he must trust in Santa Muerte, that she is going to be good to him. He took a card last time and blew it. So maybe this time he should stick with the five. He's about to put his fingers over his cards to show he doesn't want another one, when he stops. That's no way to play calavera. That's not how luck works; just because it was wrong last time doesn't make it wrong this time.

He takes a card. It's a four.

El Carnero takes a look at the two cards he has dealt himself. Since Arturo drew, El Carnero knows he must have had five or less with his first two cards. He then dealt Arturo a four, played face up for everyone to see. But that four in itself means nothing since only Arturo knows what he's already holding; a five, and with that four, he has the magic nine. He cannot be beaten. At worst, someone else might have nine and they will take back their money and replay the hand.

The nervous man and the guy with the scar have nothing.

El Carnero takes a card, and frowns. He shows a total of seven and Arturo reaches across the table and pulls four hundred American dollars toward him. It's all he can do to stop himself from screaming, but from joy or fear, he really cannot tell.

Two more wins like that and he will have the thousand. He doesn't stop to think about what two losses will do, and he takes the next bank offered: another hundred.

El Carnero watches him steadily. He deals the cards slowly and when he has, Arturo peeks at his and sees a natural nine.

—¡Calavera!—he says, flipping them over and then the fat guy laughs and says—¡Me too!

The hand is drawn and they all take back their money, and Arturo knows that's how it's going to be. She's going to make him suffer, she's going to test his faith, she's going to make him sweat for it.

They play on, and it's just as he thought.

He wins two hands, loses two. His stack of dollars creeps higher and then higher, and then he almost loses everything, and still he has to keep an empty face, for it will not do to let them know that he is desperate.

Raúl never once takes his eyes off him. Arturo can feel it, he can physically feel that he is being stared at, and that that stare is a menacing one. Life in the bar goes on. The fight that's been brewing blows into life and then the thugs on the door come and help one of the guys pound the other into a bloodied mess on the floor. The music is growling now, low and even nastier than before, and the girls on the bar are dancing hard, and they move and turn and bend and the men below them howl like hungry wolves. Arturo sees none of it.

He watches the cards come down to him and with every hand he prays to the bony girl and finally, finally, she starts to care for him again. He knows he has passed the test. She falls from the sky, she rises from the ground; wherever it is she resides, she stands behind Arturo now and directs every single card, and makes sure they all fall in exactly the right place, the right hands. She pays Arturo back for his faith, and he wins.

He wins. He wins again. And then again.

Sensing the luck has changed, El Carnero declares a bank of just fifty dollars. Arturo takes the hand and with it pulls two hundred dollars back toward him. That's it. He's done it. He doesn't need to count the money as he goes. At any moment he knows exactly how much he is up and how much he is down and what is sitting in his pocket. With that two hundred, fifty of which was his stake, he has tipped over. He has one thousand and fifty dollars, and he looks at El Carnero and, as calmly as he can, thinks, *Fuck you*.

Then he thinks something else. He has the thousand, and he's going to leave. He has the thousand, and fifty more besides and Arturo thinks that he can keep that fifty. Inside, he smiles at the thought that he won and he even made a little extra for himself. He sees it as his fee for playing, and he knows Faustino won't expect any of it. He'll just be so glad to get the thousand.

Then Arturo realizes something.

Wait a minute, he thinks. I put up fifty to play in the first place.

With this fifty, I've just broken even, and I came in here and could have gotten myself killed.

The cards have been his, they've easily been his. The Skinny Girl hasn't put a foot wrong; she's been all-powerful and impervious to the threat of these savage men. He's on a streak, and he knows it. It would be dumb, really dumb, to walk away.

—¿You in?—asks El Carnero.

Arturo nods.

The bank is a hundred, and ten seconds later Arturo has made an extra three hundred dollars.

Three hundred dollars. Even after Faustino's thousand, he has three hundred and fifty dollars. It's more money than he has ever had. Ever. He sees what he can do with it. He can buy some decent clothes, he can fix the roof, buy a heater, buy some oil. He could buy a girl a drink somewhere nice.

—¿Who's in?—El Carnero is asking, and Arturo is nodding.

—Yes. I'm in—he says, and matches the bank of fifty.

He wins again, of course.

He plays again, he wins again, and he knows nothing as it happens, he knows nothing at all, save that he suddenly realizes he has won over three thousand dollars. Three thousand dollars, only one of which he has to give to Faustino.

People crowd around the table, watching as a strange kid takes thousands of dollars off El Carnero, and the nervous guy and the guy with the scar across his head have dropped out now, but Arturo barely even knows that, as he plays on.

He thinks about his mother, and he thinks about the shack. He thinks about Faustino and he thinks about Eva and the baby. He wants something more than he has, he wants to do better, he wants to live an easier life, a better life, and right before him, right now, is the chance to do it.

Five hundred dollars will pay coyotes to get him to Los Angeles, just like Eva. He can get Siggy to tell him where to go and what to do. Siggy might even know some names, people he could stay with. If he has enough to cover the deposit on a room, he could rent his own place. He could get a job. He could work hard and find someone to love and take her to places like Western Playland.

A couple more wins and he'll have enough to do all of that, and maybe more, and Santa Muerte has been good and shown her goodness and repaid him for his faith, and then El Carnero says to the world in general—Two hundred dollars. ¿Who's in?

So Arturo says—I am.

And he loses.

It's okay, he thinks. I still have over two thousand. Just don't panic. You know how to win at calavera.

But the skull is vanity, that's all it is. It knows how to show us that everything is in vain, and all our pride and all our dreams along the way are nothing compared with that.

Arturo loses. He loses again. He feels sick. He has less than fifteen hundred dollars and after Faustino has taken his thousand, Arturo knows he has risked his life for less money than he would need to pay coyotes to get him to El Norte. So he plays on, but his head is spinning and he cannot think so clearly as before and he loses by standing on a five and then sees El Carnero deal himself a four, a *four*, which would have given Arturo nine and ¿why, why, why, he thinks, why do they use two decks?

He plays on. He plays on and loses and he's done. He's lost almost everything. He scrapes together enough for a bank of twenty and loses that too, and then El Carnero says something about lending him some money to keep playing. The people standing around the table go silent and still and one of them even wants to pull at Arturo's sleeve and tell him to get up and run, run hard, but everyone is scared of El Carnero, everyone except the White Sister, and she, it seems, has disappeared.

Arturo borrows a hundred from El Carnero, and sees it walk straight back across the table to where it came from. So he borrows two hundred, and the same thing happens to that.

He plays on and he plays on and the old gods are interested now and sit up and take notice, for they know sacrifice when they see it, and they can see bloody sacrifice coming. They erupt from the ground and circle the table, grinning. The world rips apart around the calaverita and Arturo plays on and the little skull laughs at him as he borrows and loses, borrows and loses again, until suddenly someone says—*That's enough.*

It's El Carnero who's spoken.

Arturo lifts his head.

—That's enough.

El Carnero sits back, and stretches.

—I'm tired. Game's over. Niño, you owe me four thousand dollars. But I'm a generous guy. You can have till tomorrow night to pay me back.

Arturo reels, feels the world turn over and crumble around him. He sits among its shattered pieces. He came here to play cards for Faustino's life. Not only has he lost, but he has paid with his own.

We wanted to belong. We needed to. To the world, to each other. But our greed and our fear have led us down a different path, the path to isolation. Our greed has fed our fear and our fear has fed our greed and now look where we have come: the end of the road.

It may not be the case that we are at the top of the mountain now; that we are at the pinnacle of human existence. It occurs to me that the highest point of global civilization may not be now, nor lie in some idyllic future. It may have passed, slipped by one day, unnoticed, as the world was as good as it ever will be and though we may strive to find our way back to the top of the mountain where such wonders await us, we're too late. The descent to the end has come.

GROUND ZERO

Unlike Faustino, who rode the beast from far to the south, Anapra is all Arturo has ever known. His parents came with the thousands who fled north from Durango after three years of drought. They kept moving north until, in Anapra, they slammed up against El Norte. There was no fence then; there were just concrete markers in the ground. A year later, men from America came and started to build a fence. It was primitive at first, but over the years it got bigger and stronger, yet still the fence runs out just beyond Arturo's shack.

It's been his home for about a year. Before that, he and Faustino lived in the shell of an old yellow school bus, cut off just above the wheel arches, half-buried in the ground. And before that, they lived with Arturo's parents in a jacal. If Colonia de Anapra is bad now, it was worse then. Everything was just cardboard, and scrap wood. Fires were common, but they, like everything else, fell into the pattern of life and death.

In November and December, thousands of kilometers to the south, the drugs were harvested, following which they worked their way north, and killings came with them as disputes arose and scores were settled. Through Christmas and New Year's, people hanged themselves. The first few months of the year brought death in other ways. Faulty gas heaters might poison silently in the night, with leaks of carbon monoxide, or they might explode, causing fires to rage. The spring saw fights over ground in the colonias, and, in the absence of sewer systems and good water, outbreaks of disease. In summer the water nearly ran out entirely, and there would be sporadic drug murders by the pandillas. The cool autumn would see more fights over land, and rapid building of shacks. Fires were common then too, as people stole electricity from the grid, causing short circuits that could ignite a town made of cardboard in seconds. A neighbor of Arturo's electrocuted himself trying to rig up a line; his blackening body hung from the wires for a day before men came and cut it down. Finally, winter would return, the shootings, the hangings.

This is the center of the world. It is ground zero. It is the world Arturo was born into.

His mother had to stop working in the Lear Corporation maquiladora when she became too pregnant to avoid detection, and was fired. Once Arturo had grown a little, she found work in a different factory. It was easy enough; with hundreds of the foreign-owned factories chewing their way through workers rapidly, she found a new position quickly. Every day, she would join the other workers walking to meet the company bus to the maquiladora. Often this meant leaving before dawn, while Arturo still slept, but he was old enough to look after himself by then. He was six.

Arturo's father, meanwhile, might go to work or he might not.

That depended on many things, and one of those things was how stupid he was feeling. Or how brave. Or how desperate. On days like those he would join some of the other men in the colonia and wander across into America to wait for a train to roll by. There, they would clamber aboard the moving train and use crowbars to lever their way into the boxcars, throwing down whatever looked most valuable and vanishing before the police showed up. They rarely did. For a while, the train robbing was made easier when someone found that if you connected enough car batteries to the rails it made the train's brakes fire, but the railroad got wise to that and changed their emergency systems.

It was not without its dangers. More than once, someone would fall under the train, and die. A friend of Arturo's father lost his foot, a good friend. And that was why, when skinny little Faustino turned up in Anapra one day, hobbling down the main street, begging, Arturo's mother took pity on him. For a while, things were good. Arturo had a kind of brother, his mother was working, his father wasn't drinking much. It was only when she went missing that things went wrong, and that his father went missing too, in his own way.

FREQUENTLY ASKED QUESTIONS

WHAT IS A MAQUILADORA?
A maquiladora is a Mexican assembly or manufacturing operation that can be subject to up to 100 percent non-Mexican ownership. A maquiladora utilizes competitively priced Mexican labor.

ARE MAQUILADORAS REQUIRED TO INCORPORATE MEXICAN COMPONENTS?
No. Maquiladoras are not required to use any Mexican components in assembly processing or manufacturing.

WHAT ARE THE MEXICAN TARIFF/DUTY POLICIES RELATING TO THIS PROGRAM?
As long as the imported components brought into Mexico are destined for export, no Mexican import duty is levied on them.

WHAT ARE THE ADVANTAGES OF THE MAQUILADORA PROGRAM?
Low labor costs
Trainable workforce
Proximity to US market and distribution centers
Cooperative, nonunion workforce
Fine quality of life for US managers living in El Paso

THE DELIVERER

No one looks at Arturo.

He staggers away to find the bathroom, to clean himself up. The water splutters out into Arturo's hands, and he splashes it over his head, takes a long drink from the tap. The bathroom door opens and Raúl walks in, props himself against a filthy sink. His sleeves are rolled up. He is covered in gang markings, and there, just as on Faustino's arm, is the tattoo of Santa Muerte.

—¿You weren't thinking of going no place?

It's not really a question. Arturo sees Raúl nod at the little window, which is covered with heavy bars.

—I'm kidding—says Raúl.—You can go any time you want. Only, El Carnero wants to see you first. ¿Right?

Arturo wipes his face on his sleeves, straightens.

He nods and not, making eye contact, passes Raúl, heading toward the door.

He's almost there when Raúl speaks again.

—Hey. One thing. You know he's messing with you. ¿Right?

Arturo doesn't understand.

—¿What do you mean?

—He knows you don't got four thousand dollars. No. Anyway, four thousand dollars is nothing to him. It's just a game, pendejo. It's just a game. And you've already lost.

Arturo fights the urge to run and walks back into the bar, which is emptying out. It's late. There's still music but it's old-time mariachi now, incongruous. El Carnero is still sitting at the table, alone. He sees Arturo and beckons him over with a finger, points to the chair.

—¿You said you're from Anapra?

Arturo nods. He cannot look at El Carnero; it is like looking at the face of the sun. He could be burned to a cinder just by trying it, the power is so great. Arturo knows that if he looks at this man then he will be looking at his future, and it is not good.

—Yeah, I thought so. Anapra. So I can do you a little favor. Give you a ride home.

—No—says Arturo.—No, I have, I mean, I can—

El Carnero cuts him off.

—It's no trouble. You see, Raúl has some business that way anyway. Tonight. He's bringing his truck around right now. And then I thought, I'll come with you too. Give you a lift home. So I know where to come and get my dollars, tomorrow. ¿Right?

No, thinks Arturo. No. No, no, no. Faustino is waiting in his car on Calle Libertad. But he cannot say that, he just has to get away from here somehow.

—No—says Arturo.—I'll tell you where I live, but—

—Good—says El Carnero, taking absolutely no notice of him at all.—There's Raúl outside. Let's go.

El Carnero gets up, pulling a jacket from the back of his chair, which he slings over his shoulder.

—The nights are cold now—he says.—¿Right?

Arturo nods, noticing that El Carnero limps as he walks, just the same way Faustino does. They leave the bar, the heavies on the door nodding to El Carnero as he passes.

The red pickup is outside. There are three men in the back, narcos. One of them has tattoos all across his face like Rául does, only these are even stranger: he has had his face turned into a skull. The tip of his nose has been blacked out, his eyes are blackened skull-like sockets; skeletal teeth have even been tattooed across his lips. Arturo pulls his gaze away from this man as El Carnero gives him a soft shove in the back, pointing him toward the cab of the truck. Raúl's in the driver's seat. El Carnero walks up to the door and opens it.

—I'm driving—he says.—The kid's up front with me.

Arturo thinks that maybe Raúl hesitates, just for a moment. Not enough to really see, not enough to upset El Carnero. He climbs down from the cab and walks to the back of the truck, where he climbs up into the bed using the wheel as a step.

—Get in—El Carnero says, and Arturo clambers into the cab, and as he does so, he makes the mistake of glancing back through the small rear window. He sees the three men looking at him, and Raúl saying something to them. Something about him. He notices they all have guns. Two of them have small folding automatic rifles. But he sees something else, something worse. It's dark, there are few lights in the street, but it seems that lying on the bed of the truck, between the four men, is a shape; long and bulky. Motionless.

El Carnero fires up the engine.

He turns to Arturo.

—¿You hear something? I don't. Raúl is like a mother with a baby. This damn truck. There's always something wrong with it. Only it's all in his head. ¿You hear something? I don't, but maybe you do. You're a mechanic. ¿Right?

Arturo shakes his head.

—No, I'm not a mechanic. I just haul stuff around the yard.

—Okay, okay, but tell me what you think. ¿It sound okay to you?

Arturo nods.—Yes.

El Carnero pulls away.

—Here's what we're gonna do. I'm gonna drive you to your place. And on the way, we're going to have a chat. ¿That sound good?

Arturo nods.

—I said, ¿Does that sound good?

There's a touch of irritation in his voice that scares Arturo.

—Yeah—he says quickly.—Yeah. Sounds good.

They drive.

El Alacrán may have been winding down, but Juárez is only just getting started. They tear through the streets. As terrified as Arturo is, the world looks different from inside the cab of a truck like this, a powerful truck, with tinted windows and black leather seats. They're high up, level with or above the heads of most people in the streets, and it feels good somehow. Arturo is too scared to think about why it feels good, he just senses it, sensing something that thousands of other weak, poor young kids before him have

126

sensed, and been attracted to. For there is a drug here. It's a different kind of drug than the one that El Carnero and his like make money from, so much money, by selling to the users of El Norte. This drug, which Arturo barely senses, is the leather seats of the truck, it's the tinted windows, it's the guns in the narcos' hands, it's the rolls of dollars in their pockets. This drug is the most powerful drug of them all; its effects are both fast and powerful. Arturo looks through the tinted windows of the truck; he sees people in the streets taking great care not to look at them, pretending that the truck doesn't exist. That was him until a very short time ago.

There is no room for such thoughts right now. All Arturo can think is how stupid he's been, how dumb. How he got greedy, how he broke all his rules, how wrong this all is, when he didn't ask for it to happen. It was Faustino. Faustino marched back into his life with his bunch of problems, and made them his own. A year ago, Arturo wouldn't have blinked before helping, he would have done anything for his friend, his brother. But that was before Faustino left. He didn't owe Faustino anything, Arturo thinks, So why has he let himself get into this mess?

On top of all this, El Carnero is speaking to him, easily now, calmly, chatting away like he's Arturo's uncle, about this, and that, and then he says—¿You know a kid called Faustino?

—¿Faustino?—Arturo asks, desperately trying to play innocent.

—Yeah, Faustino. He's one of mine. He's from Anapra. I mean he was. Not anymore, but he's about your age. I thought maybe you know him.

—No, I don't know anyone called Faustino.

—¿No? ¿You sure? It's a common enough name. ¿Right?

—Yes, I guess it is. But I don't know him.

Arturo's mind tries to speed ahead of the conversation; to seek out the gaps; spot the pitfalls, watch for the traps that El Carnero is setting for him, and all the time it's doing that, Arturo's mind is also thinking that El Carnero cannot know they know each other. Faustino and him. Unless maybe Faustino's spoken about his past, about his friends, back in Anapra. Maybe he—

—¿What's your name, niño?

So now Arturo has a split second to decide whether to tell the truth, or not, but before he can decide, he finds that he has opened his goddamn mouth and spoken anyway.

—Arturo.

Arturo waits for the killer blow. He stares through the windshield, waiting for El Carnero to reach over and slam his head into the dash, or shove him against the door and put a bullet through his face. Just for lying.

—Oh—says El Carnero.—Arturo. I like that name. Like the king. ¿Right?

Arturo does not have the faintest idea what he is talking about, but he knows that he is still alive, and that must mean that Faustino never mentioned him. He feels both relieved and hurt. So Faustino walked out of their life and into a new one and never once mentioned his best friend?

Juárez passes by, and here, at once both safe and in appalling danger, Arturo sees the city as he has never seen it before.

It is alive, writhing and strong. On every corner, on every street, in every bar, deals are going down. People with blank faces that nevertheless reek of their desperation push their way through the world, hunting for what they need, what they need, what they know they really need. Questions are asked and people greet each other, flirting, laughing, crying, shouting. Money changes hands, drugs change hands. Guns are being loaded, guns are being used.

As they reach Azucenas, at the corner where the bridge to El Paso is just meters away, they hear the sound of shooting. Arturo looks and sees a car doing a U-turn and then screeching away, heading out of sight. People are standing around something on the ground, outside the drugstore.

There are shadows in every alley, every doorway, and the lights of shops and bars and signs and cars dazzle and blind and make the shadows darker still. In those shadows lurk the fierce gods of our past, the desperate gods of our future who know we have been running away, simply trying to escape them, for all these hundreds of years. They know that time is running out; that it will not be long, and Juárez is the proof of that.

As they turn a corner, one of the men in the back knocks on the glass and shakes his head, shouts something through the window that Arturo doesn't quite catch. He's shaking a walkie-talkie, show-ing he was just told something over the radio.

El Carnero takes a turn, puts them on a different street.

—Las Panteras down that way.—he says, nodding toward where they've come from.—And we don't want trouble tonight. Any other night, we might want trouble, but not tonight. Tonight we just want to get you home safe. ¿Right?

Arturo stares and stares and the city smears its way past his eyes.

—This town . . .—says El Carnero.—I'm old enough to remember when there was some kind of order here; the cartel ruled everyone, and that was that. No one controls these streets anymore. Now it's just anarchy; total and all-out war between all-comers. It's Hell, plain and simple, and that's funny because you know what they say—"Even the Devil is scared of living in Juárez." But not me. It doesn't matter where you go; you have to die somewhere. ¿Right?

Right, thinks Arturo. Right. Right, right, right.

He thinks about the shape in the back of the truck, lying on the floor between the four men, something long and bulky and wrapped in plastic, bound with black tape. He thinks about what business El Carnero could possibly have in Anapra at two in the morning, and he thinks about Gabriel, who ran the hardware store, till five o'clock this afternoon.

No temas a donde vayas, que haz de morir donde debes.

They ride.

Juárez is left behind as they climb up toward the sierra, and Anapra.

—¿Which way, niño?—El Carnero asks, at every intersection, and Arturo can do nothing but tell the truth.

—Right—he says, as they reach Pulpo, another of the beasts of the sea, and then they are pulling up outside Arturo's shack, and he realizes this is his last chance to beg for his life.

—Please, you have to understand. This is where I live. ¡Look! I don't have four thousand dollars. Please. I'll pay you back, somehow, but you have to understand. I don't have any money.

El Carnero listens, showing no emotion at all.

—Please—Arturo begs—I don't have any dollars, I don't have any money at all.

—I know you don't—El Carnero says, and then he's fishing around in his jacket pocket and Arturo thinks, Let it be quick, but then he sees that El Carnero has pulled out his phone.

He holds it up.

The flash blinds Arturo's eyes.

He's still blinking, trying to see, as El Carnero says—Just in case you decide to run. You know you can't. ¿Right? I send this to the boys in Barrio Azteca, they send it everywhere else. Everywhere in Chihuahua, everywhere in Texas, everywhere in California. Everywhere. ¿You understand? I know you do. I'll be back tomorrow for my cash, around sunset. Now get out of here, we have work to do.

Arturo stumbles from the cab, the afterburn of the camera flash still blinding him, so that he cracks his head on the lintel of his door as he makes his way in.

He staggers to his bed in the dark, and lies down, and for a while he can think nothing. He is empty, he is gone. His body is no more than a shell; for breathing, for holding his pounding heart somewhere while it beats its last few beats on this earth.

He senses something warm on his face and, feeling his skull, finds that he's bleeding from where he cracked it on the doorway. He holds his fingers there for a while, nausea and exhaustion sweeping into him in powerful ocean waves, stronger and stronger each time, and his head is swimming, trying to swim, to climb out of the black waters, but this darkness is something he cannot fight.

There are sounds outside, from the sierra, from the no-man's-land between here and El Norte. Then the shooting starts. Cracks of pistol fire and the stammering of automatic weapons. Distant shouts come down from the hill, but despite it all, Arturo is utterly exhausted.

He sleeps.

ARTURO'S DREAM

Arturo dreams a dream that lasts for centuries.

He hovers above the ground—this, the center of the world—and looks down from the starry heavens upon his own form, lying still on his bed. It is a pure, clear Mexican desert night, and the sky is an indigo sheet and the diamond stars are the eyes of apocalyptic monsters who have spent millions of years waiting for this moment, when everything on this corrosive earth is ready, when everything is aligned just so; when the world is ready to burn.

For now, all is calm. The distant hills to the north are a page of black paper set against the sky, and the glow of the conjoined and deformed twins that are Juárez and El Paso tinges a few nighttime clouds with dirty orange.

In Anapra, the beasts of the sea sense that the time has come. They erupt from their dirt tracks and begin to swim up and down the streets that bear their names, a few feet off the ground, swimming easily through the air. A salmon here, crossing with the shark. Fish of all kinds: turbot and bream, and carp, intersecting with the conger eel, the octopus. Then Arturo realizes that they are not the fish themselves he can see, but merely their letters, their names, which are swimming. The word *salmón* glides past a scuttling crab. A whale lumbers beside a shoal of small, flickering sardines.

Still all is calm, and then, something drops from the high heavens where Arturo looks down at the world. It is something burning, a rag. It is a rag dipped in gasoline; burning, incendiary. It takes minutes to fall from the sky, minute after minute, quite beautiful; tumbling, flaming, sparking, fuming black smoke in the blackness, and then it touches the ground, and Anapra erupts into a fireball.

Everything is alight, everything burns. The houses burn and the hospital burns and the gas station burns and the firestorm is so intense that even the ground itself begins to burn. Arturo sees people running from their homes, and their clothes are on fire, and their skin and their hair, and their eyes are on fire and their hearts are on fire, and they are screaming but Arturo sees that he is still lying in his bed, peaceful, calm.

Arturo looks away from the burning people. He wonders about the sea creatures. As he gazes down from his dizzying height, he is surprised to see that they are untouched by the fire, and they swim on through the flames as if they were water, and then he thinks, That's to be expected; they are only words, after all, but then he sees something else.

Distracted by the inferno, he has not noticed that the few clouds in the sky have grown, that they are even now multiplying and spreading across the sky. They're tall and weighty clouds, towering up above the mountains, looming, and then with a sudden crack and beat, lightning skewers the world; a single bolt that splits into three as it penetrates and there is a long silence then; long, empty and full of threat, after which the thump of the thunder shakes the ground, disturbing old things that would be better left to rot.

On that stroke, the rain comes.

It is a storm like no other since the forging of the world, and water hammers down from the sky, and even the furnace that is Anapra burning cannot resist it. The flames are extinguished, and in their place, the water rises.

The world drowns now, as Arturo looks on. He sees the burned bodies of his neighbors vanish under the surface of the rising water, sees their burned mouths fill with water as they disappear from sight; he sees the fish swimming in their true habitat, content at last, real animals now, no longer just words, and the rain falls, falls, falls and that word, now that it is in Arturo's mind, can be ignored no longer as he understands that there is no way he can hover in the sky, that he is standing on nothing, that he is clinging to nothing.

He falls, tumbling toward the water, which is swallowing the earth. Just like the burning rag, it takes him minutes to fall, and the water is rising at an ever-increasing rate, so that now only the summit of Mount Cristo Rey is visible.

Arturo sees that he is falling toward himself, still lying motion-less in the bed where he is dreaming and he breaks the surface of the sea and plunges down and into himself and then his eyes jerk open and he breathes lungful after lungful of water. Desperate for life, desperate for *birth*, he claws his way through the broken roof of his shack and soars up out of the water and into the sky, landing on the slopes of the hill where, above him, Christ stands with his arms outstretched, forgiving everyone.

Arturo climbs the mountain and takes his place. He steps inside the figure of Jesus the King and, cursing everyone, he holds his arms out wide. Like a radio antenna, he begins to collect. From the twin cities beneath him, from Anapra, from Mexico, from America, he collects.

Words, sentences, phrases, thoughts, fears, desires. He pulls them all into him, and they are conversations and essays and dreams. They are websites and they are novels. They are racist rants in cyberspace and they are biased media reports. They are messages from narco-lords scrawled in blood on bedsheets and they are bigoted tirades of presidential candidates. They are the rattled thoughts of the dying addict, the undoubting proclamations of the religious leader. They are prayers, statistics, beliefs, opinions, ideas and verdicts and aspirations and judgments; they are hate and hope and they come at him in Spanish and English and a bastard mixture of the two, mestizo.

The voices tumble into Arturo, King Arturo, and every one hurts him, every single one gives him pain and he curses them all but he forgives them all too, and the voices shout and fight, they agree and disagree, but no matter what they say, no matter who they are, no matter where they come from, they are all saying the one and same thing.

¿What have we lost? ¿What have we lost?

DEATH AND THE IDEA OF MEXICO

As Arturo wakes from his dream, he immediately knows that one person was absent from it. The bony girl, the beautiful one. Santa Muerte has abandoned him, he knows, but then, he knew that last night as the fatal cards came down. She has abandoned him, and maybe he should never have asked her for help, maybe she is too demanding. Or, just maybe, he didn't pray hard enough, he is not devout enough, and perhaps there is still time to prove himself to her, and the world.

He sits up and from nowhere his head throbs so badly it makes him reel. His fingers gingerly find the place on his skull where he cracked his head and he feels a scab forming and blood, still sticky. He doesn't really remember his dream, just snatches of it. His mind is on other things, he feels lousy, as if hung over from the fear. He gets up and goes to wash his head, leaving a small plastic dish of blood-reddened water behind. He stumbles out into the cold morning.

It is early, and he shivers, but the sun is up and begins to warm him and then he turns and sees Mount Cristo Rey and he sees Christ the King, and with that, his dream comes back to him, all of it.

It means nothing.

It means nothing. There are only two things that matter. The first is that he is dead. As good as. The second thing is that there was gunfire in the night, on the high sierra. Gunfire, and he doesn't know what it means; whether it was a war between gangs, or a gang in a shootout with the police, which is more or less the same thing, or the Americans, but he prays it wasn't a gang of pollos, and if it was, he hopes that the people Eva and the baby were crossing with were using someplace else.

He thinks she's probably okay. Coyotes don't use Cristo Rey so much anymore. He's heard some stories about tunnels to the east of Juárez, and someone told him about the cattle market a few kilometers to the west of Anapra. He forgets the name, but it's a big place, with cattle pens on both the Mexican and American sides of the border, just feet from each other, and they have their own border crossing, a border crossing for livestock only, except during the hours of darkness, when the night guards take a share of the coyotes' fee to turn a blind eye to some human traffic. It's supposed to be one of the safest places to cross and will stay that way until some official or high-ranking policeman stops taking his sobre, his envelope, to forget it's happening. And you don't stop taking your envelope because the alternative to that is a bullet. Arturo hopes Eva went that way.

He's struck by thirst and hunger and goes back inside to take a long drink of water. From under his bed he pulls out a plastic tub, and snapping off the lid he eats the last of the tortillas he has been keeping. He chews them without thinking, without feeling. He will find some better food later; for now he just needs something to stop his hunger, so he can think.

He thinks about the task before him, and he knows it is almost impossible. He thinks about running, but as tempting as that idea seems, he knows that it is foolish, and pointless. He has no money, nowhere to go, no one to hide him, no papers. The desert is wide and the cities even more hostile for someone like him. And *they* are everywhere. If he runs, they will kill him once they find him whether he has the money or not, because it will no longer be about the money, but about their twisted ideas of honor.

Arturo thinks about Faustino, and wonders what he thought when he never showed up. He wonders if something has happened to him, or whether he will turn up any second, wanting to know if he's been saved.

Arturo knows that he has not saved his friend. Worse than that, he had the thousand in his hands, he could have walked, he *should* have walked, he should have *run* out of there and through the streets to find Faustino. He didn't. He saw the chance to become someone better, and, greedily, he went after it, and in doing so he has doomed them both. Yet Faustino still has a day to find his thousand dollars, which is better odds than Arturo has, for he has a day to find four thousand.

No, he thinks. I must find five. I must find four for me and one for Faustino. It's my fault, it's my fault. We could be laughing about it all now, but it's my fault. We could be sitting in luxury in his place on Calle Libertad and laughing about it, but we're not, and it's my fault.

Instead, he has to achieve the almost impossible, but there is one little thing that is keeping him going, and that is the word *almost*. Almost impossible, almost, and that word gives him the slightest chance, and the slightest hope. He knows people in Anapra; there are good people, people who try to live well, live normal lives, people who want nothing to do with the drugs, and the violence that goes with them. There are people he knows who might have some dollars stashed away. Maybe he can borrow and beg his way to survival.

He's about to leave when he thinks again about Faustino. ¿What if he comes while I'm out? He needs to get moving, but he must get in touch with Faustino somehow, must at least leave him a note of some kind. Quickly, he hunts around the shack for something to write with, something to write on. He does not have these things. In the end the best he can find is his pack of calavera cards and a ballpoint that does not work. He experiments a little and finds that he can just about scrawl letters by dipping the tip of the ballpoint into the water that is heavily tainted with his blood.

He chooses the four aces since they have the most white space on which to write and then he stops, wondering what he should say.

He thinks about what happened. He thinks about what El Carnero said about sunset. He thinks about the task ahead of him. Then he writes.

On the first ace, he writes: *F—Sorry.*

On the second: *Still trying.*

On the third: *Meet me here at five.*

On the fourth, on the fourth . . .

On the fourth card he hesitates, for a long, long time, then he thinks, *¡Cabrón!* and without thinking any more he writes, carefully and steadily, in his own blood: *I love you. A.*

He shuts the door to his shack. It has a beveled edge reinforcing its flimsy surface. This surround is coming away and there's a tiny crack into which he slips the edges of the four playing cards, one above the other, at eye height, face out. Faustino will see them. He will be able to read them, Arturo hopes, though the blood and water mix is faint and fading already as it dries in the morning sunlight.

Faustino will read them. He will return at five, by which time Arturo will have found four, no *five* thousand dollars, and he will give Faustino his money, and they will both be saved.

Arturo sets off, walking fast down Salmón and then taking Ballena and Sìluro in order to avoid the hill at the top of Cangrejo.

He's at the point where Sìluro crosses the lower end of Cangrejo, when a truck comes crawling over the ridge of that hill. He sees it's a federal police truck, a dark-blue pickup with a roll cage on the back. There are two guys in the cab, as always, and four behind, all wearing bulletproof jackets and face masks. They hold their guns slung toward the ground, and Arturo does not look at them as they edge by him. He feels their stares on the back of his neck, but he keeps his head down and he keeps walking and then, as it passes him, the truck picks up speed heading toward Rancho Anapra.

Two minutes later he finds out why.

He sees the truck parked behind two others on the main street, right outside Gabriel's store. There are cops standing around and a small crowd of people. There are shouts and he sees a woman screaming and yelling at one of the policemen. Each time she shoves him away, she falls wailing to the ground behind her and crouches over something lying in the street. Arturo sees what that something is: a long heavy bundle wrapped in white plastic and bound with tape. She's pawing at the plastic and people are pulling her away and the cop is shouting at her while others are speaking into radios. From time to time she gets up again and yells at the cop some more, pushing him away and telling him to leave, that they're not welcome.

As Arturo comes closer he hears what the cop is saying. He's snapping orders at the people gathered around, snapping and ordering Gabriel's widow to stand away, that she is *tampering with evidence.*

—¡Evidence!—she shouts.—¿What evidence? ¡Evidence that you are incompetent, that you are useless! ¡Corrupt! ¡Go away! ¡Go away and leave us alone!

Arturo knows who did this to Gabriel, and his wife. He does not stop walking. For a split second he sees himself walking up to one of the cops to tell them he knows that it was El Carnero and his gang who did it, and that he can tell them where they can be found. He knows it will do no good, almost certainly. He has no faith in the police, no one does; the chances of finding a cop who isn't corrupt are not good enough to take the risk of putting yourself in the hands of one who's in the pay of the gangs. At worst, he will get himself implicated in the murder; at best, it will do nothing but waste his time on a day when he has none to spare. Either way, it will not bring Gabriel back from the dead, and that is the only thing that his wife really wants, the thing she cannot have.

He walks on, turns up Tiburón, heading for José's auto shop. Behind him is the house he has been very careful not to look at: Doña Maria's, home to the shrine to Santa Muerte. Arturo sees himself from the night before, slipping the money into his shoe, and just as quickly he tries to block that image in his mind. He finds he cannot. It does not even occur to him to ask himself if he actually believes in her, or not. She is there, that's all he knows. She's everywhere. All that matters is that he has a day to prove whether she is still on his side or whether he is going to pay the price for cheating her, or, he thinks, *trying* to cheat her. Because no one cheats death in the end. She is the skull, the calavera. She is the white bone and charcoal eye, she is the one waiting to act as deliverer, and she does not discriminate; she chooses rich and poor and good and bad alike, and she does not even ask that you come to find her. *She* will seek *you* out, when the time comes; so do not fear where you go, for death will find you wherever you are, and deliver you from this earth to the next.

Arturo walks on, a little faster, putting Gabriel's body behind him. He's trying not to think about the large amount of blood seeping from the plastic, trying not to think what that probably means: that it was not swift. He tries not to think about how long it took, or what they did. Back there, on the corner, Gabriel's wife is still screaming, but as Arturo walks on into the distance, her screams fade.

Nations are like people: first, they are born, they become children, they behave like children. They fight, they explore. They become adolescent. They fight even more but maybe they begin to understand. They might even become adults for a short time. But it's important to remember that the process of civilization does not only work in one direction. Having reached adulthood, nations get even older; they forget, they become senile. And so, civilization starts to crumble, and once-great empires become debased, violent and die. They destroy themselves.

It's true.

Nations are like people.

The migrants from the south and from Mexico heading to America. They are a sign. Refugees from Africa and the Middle East heading for Europe. They are a sign. Migrants from Southeast Asia trying to get to Australia. They are all unwitting messengers, and their message is this: We are just the tip of the iceberg. Though iceberg is the wrong word, because it's when the icebergs melt, and the world changes forever, that the migration we see today will look like nothing. Nothing. Then all civilizations will crumble. It will be biblical. It will be apocalyptic.

THE ANALYSIS
OF THE EGO

Arturo finds José under the hood of a white Chevy that has seen better days. He sticks his head out for long enough to complain to Arturo that he is late for work, and to listen while Arturo tells him he is not coming to work today, and that in fact, he needs José's help.

Five minutes later, Arturo is halfway across Anapra, José's mocking laughter still in his ears. He didn't even get as far as saying why he needs five thousand dollars, José just began laughing when he asked him for money, and when Arturo said it was dollars that he needed, and five thousand of them, he got nasty.

Arturo told him what he thought of him, and then he quit. He told José he wasn't coming back, so he could find someone else to whine at every day. It feels like a small victory to Arturo. The feeling only lasts a few minutes, but while it does, he feels better for having taken some control in his life. He told someone else how he wanted things to be, not the other way around, and though the conscious thought has worn off, it's left something significant behind in Arturo.

In his head is a list of people he can try to ask for the money. It is, in truth, a very short list, and José has just been removed from it. Now, Arturo heads toward somewhere he knows he will find a better reception: El Diván.

Bar by night, El Diván runs as a simple cantina by day, cooking up basic things for the workers of Anapra. On Saturday morning, it is always quiet, and today is no exception.

Arturo climbs up the steps and goes to open the door, and finds it locked. He peers through but can see no one.

He bangs on the door, and bangs on it again.

—¡Hola!—he cries, but there is no reply.

He hesitates. His time is short, but Siggy and Carlos are probably his best hope. Unsure whether to come back later, or wait, he flops down on the abused sofa that sits on the stoop. Cars come and go, a black sedan with a roll of insulation poking out of the rear window, a white pickup with four guys in overalls dozing in the back, off to a job somewhere. A woman walks with two little kids down the sidewalk, she nods at Arturo. He nods back, then shuts his eyes.

¿Is it possible? he thinks. ¿Is it possible that, just yesterday morning, none of this had happened? It cannot be possible. Time cannot work that way; and life cannot go from bearable to fatal in such a short moment of time. He knows he's wrong, of course. It happened for Gabriel, last night. And for Gabriel's wife, now his widow. Her name comes to him: Ana. She's sold him things in the past, when Gabriel wasn't around.

Ana. Arturo wonders what he will say to her if he ever goes in there again, and whether he will go to the police after all, and tell them who did this terrible thing to her husband. Then, just as he's wondering if there will be a next time, he hears footsteps inside El Diván, and after some rattling, the door opens. Carlos sticks his head out, grinning.

—¡Arturo! ¿Come to pay us another visit?

Arturo nods.

—Carlos. ¿Is Siggy up? I need to talk to you both.

Carlos looks hard at Arturo. He's not smiling anymore.

—Give me five minutes. ¿You want some breakfast? Get off the couch and come on in.

Carlos waves Arturo in and then locks the door behind them again.

—We don't want to open just yet—he explains to Arturo.— Siggy had too much last night. Worst person in the world to run a bar. I'll go find him. You put some coffee on.

Carlos points over behind the counter where there's a hotplate and pot. Arturo wanders around and starts to fix the coffee, and by the time it's ready, Siggy stumbles out into the deserted bar and lifts a weak hand in greeting to Arturo. He looks terrible. Still unshaven, with long, white stubble; his eyes are begging to shut, but he's out of bed, he's here.

Despite everything, Arturo grins, and shoves a big mug of coffee over the bar to Siggy.

—This might help—he says, and somehow, just the act of handing over the coffee makes him feel a little better too.

—Carlos said you want to talk.

Arturo nods as Carlos comes back into the bar.

—¿That trouble didn't go away?

And Arturo shakes his head.

—Food first—says Carlos.—I'll make some eggs. We're not going to talk trouble on an empty stomach. That goes for you too, *cabrón*.

He points a wooden spoon at Siggy and then breaks into a smile and Arturo thinks how nice it must be, to be the two of them, and to run a place like this. And they fight sometimes but they have each other and they serve food and pour drinks and make people feel better than they did when they walked in. That must be nice, Arturo thinks. That must be very nice.

So Carlos makes scrambled eggs, a huge pile of eggs, and sprinkles it with pimiento and brings the whole lot over with some tortillas and the coffee pot. There, at a table by the window, the three of them eat.

Carlos wolfs his food down, Siggy picks at his, and Arturo eats slowly, forcing himself to eat forkful by forkful, because though he does not feel hungry he knows he will need the energy before the day is done, and when they're finished, Arturo tells them everything. He tells them everything about Faustino and Los Libertadores, and he tells them about the game, and the money, and he tells them he has to find five thousand dollars by five o'clock.

Siggy and Carlos look at each other and then they look at Arturo, with a deep sadness written across both their faces, as Carlos explains that they do have some money, but that they have pesos, not dollars, and even with all they have, they do not begin to have enough to change into five thousand American dollars. Of that, gringo money, Carlos explains, they have very little.

—I think we have maybe five hundred stashed away somewhere—he says.—They're yours, if they are any help at all . . .

Arturo hears what they say, but it takes a while to sink in. They were his best hope, he knows. So I'm dead, he thinks. I'm dead, I'm dead, I'm dead. He stares across the deserted bar for a while, as Siggy and Carlos exchange glances. Carlos widens his eyes at his friend, and Siggy knows what he means. Do something, say something.

Siggy coughs, clears his throat.

—You know, Arturo. You're our very good friend. If there's anything else we can do for you, you know . . .

He trails off. Carlos is shaking his head and all three of them know full well that the only thing Arturo needs right now is five thousand dollars.

Arturo nods. But I'm dead, I'm dead, I'm dead.

—Yes, I know—he says, somehow.—Thank you. Keep your five hundred. God knows you've earned it.

He starts to get up but Carlos puts his hand on his arm, gestures at the chair.

—Sit, Arturo. Finish your coffee before you go. You need it.

—No—says Arturo.—I'm fine. I just have to get going. I'm fine.

Siggy points at Arturo.

—Arturo. You are not fine. That is a lie, but the first person a liar lies to is himself. So admit it. You are not fine. Give yourself a moment. With us. Talk to us.

Arturo nods, and sits down again, and suddenly Siggy slams his hand on the table so hard it makes Carlos and Arturo jump.

—¡Damn it!—he snaps.—¡Damn it all!

Carlos tries to comfort him, calm him down, but Arturo can see that Siggy is on the verge of one of his rants. He holds up his hands and tries to calm himself down, but ends up shaking his head angrily.

—To hell with it—he says.—Arturo, my poor friend. ¿What words can be said to console you? Look at us all; all of us. Everyone. We all struggle to achieve a long life, to avoid death. ¿But finally, what good is a long life if it is difficult and barren of joys, and if it is so full of misery that we can only welcome death as a deliverer?

Carlos pulls a face at Arturo, but strangely, Arturo smiles. He smiles at his friends.

—Siggy—he says.—You're a good man. You have Carlos. And you're so clever, I wish I was like you. ¿But why are you so sad?

Siggy looks up, blinking, not expecting such a question from their young friend. He laughs a short, hard laugh and then spreads his arms out wide.

—Look around you—he says.—Look at the world. Look at what people do to one another.

—People do good things too—says Carlos, then he turns to Arturo.—Siggy and I disagree about certain matters. I believe in community. In togetherness. That we can help each other. But Siggy believes that people only serve themselves.

—¿Is that true?—asks Arturo.

—It's not their fault—Siggy says.—Not all the time. And sometimes, maybe small acts of self-sacrifice are possible.

—Like right now—says Arturo.—You would have lent me the money. If you had it. ¿Right?

Siggy nods.

—Yes, my friend. Of course. But maybe we would only have done so to feel good about ourselves. Ultimately we would just have been serving ourselves.

Carlos shakes his head sadly.

—¡Always so complicated!—he says.—¡Always so negative! You say we should look around us; but here, in Anapra, people are doing good things. Look at Las Hormigas, at the things they've managed, despite everything.

Arturo agrees with Carlos. Las Hormigas, the community organization known as the Ants, has worked hard on the little colony of Anapra, striving to make things better: getting kids educated, getting women to the factories safely, providing therapy for people who've suffered, and there are enough of those in Anapra.

—A drop in the ocean—says Siggy.—And I say that with no joy, with no satisfaction. I ask you to look around, at what Juárez is, what it *really* is. There is a fence being built here, but it is not the fence of steel and wire you see over there.

He waves his hand toward the north.

—It is *a wall* that is being built. And these are the bricks in the wall: the drug gangs, the police of Mexico and of America, Migra, the DEA, the governments and politicians of these two countries. Then there are the biggest bricks of all: companies; these giant corporations that are more powerful than anything, more powerful even than the countries where they operate. The maquiladoras here; they pay no taxes. *None.* They pay wages so low that even a job still means living on the poverty line. ¿And why does this happen? Our leaders; they tell us that this capitalism of theirs will save the world, that it will create jobs so that everyone will get richer. ¡It's a lie! ¿How can there be a consumer society when its workers do not earn enough to *consume* anything?

Carlos tries to interrupt, but Siggy will not be stopped now.

—These are the bricks in a wall that is being built not just here, but across the world. ¿And who are we? We are the mortar that is squeezed between the bricks of the wall. We are the ones who glue them together. And when the wall is finished, on one side will be the rich, and on the other, the poor. ¡So a small number of rich people get richer, and the rest can go to hell!

Siggy thumps the table again, and Carlos reaches out toward his friend.

—Siggy, be calm. I agree with you, you know that. But calm down. It's not good for you. And Arturo doesn't want to hear—

—No—says Arturo.

He turns to Siggy. He knows he doesn't have the time for this. He knows he has to go out into the streets and find five thousand dollars. But he also knows that the chances of doing that are extremely slim, and if this is his last day on earth, if this is to be the last time he sees his friends, he wants more of it. Greedily, he trades his chances of surviving for a few more minutes with Siggy and Carlos. It's another wager, but Arturo finds it's one that's surprisingly easy to make.

—I do want to hear—he says.—Really. Siggy, last night you were going to tell me something. Something about you. You said only Carlos knows who you are. ¿What did you mean?

Siggy looks at Carlos, as if seeking permission.

Carlos holds up his hands.

—¡Very well!—he says.—But be calm, my friend. Be calm.

Siggy catches his breath. He laughs, shaking his head, smiling at Carlos. As the sun climbs and moves, light slides sideways into El Diván, slowly spreading shadows of the bars on the windows across the floor. As they talk, the bars creep toward Arturo, fraction by fraction.

—Last night, I was going to tell you something I learned, long ago.

Arturo nods.

—Go on.

—Everyone here calls me El Alemán. The German. ¿Right? ¡But I am not even German! My parents came from Austria. We moved to the States when I was small and they were well off and I was a spoiled little brat. This was in LA. I dropped out of school and I did some stupid things, and then I got addicted to drugs. Yes, now I drink too much, but back then, I was a user. Of cocaine, weed. Other stuff. My parents disowned me, but I had enough money for a time and I sank lower and lower into the lowest pits of America and I couldn't stop using the drugs. And one day, I met my dealer and I said something to him I'd heard on the radio that day, someone going on about Mexicans coming over the border and taking our jobs. I didn't even think for myself; I just repeated what I'd heard this guy saying on the radio. ¿And you know what the dealer said?

Arturo waits, shaking his head. Siggy takes a sip of coffee and then pours more for all three of them.

—This is what he said: *¿You know why some come here? They come here to escape a drug war that is fueled by you.* That is fueled by you. He meant me, and others like me; because if no one was using drugs, there would be no one to sell them to. And then the drug wars would be over.

—But that's never going to happen—Arturo says.—People are weak. Drugs make them feel better. For a while at least.

155

—Yes—says Carlos.—And by then, it's too late. But Arturo, I don't think it's because people are weak. I think it's because they are scared.

Siggy's nodding at what Carlos has just said.

—¿Scared?—Arturo asks.—¿What are they scared of?

But even before Carlos can answer, Arturo knows what he's going to say.

—Everything, Arturo. They're scared of everything.

Arturo shakes his head.

—¿Can that be true?

—¿Why not?—asks Siggy.—It may be horrific, but that doesn't make it any less true. The world as we find it is a lie. A lie made between those with power: those who run the companies, those who run the government, and those who control the police and the army. I think they believe their own lie. And this is what I learned: that most of us believe it too. The first person a liar lies to is himself. ¿Right? But we are part of it, this lie, and meanwhile, we are eaten up, even as we help the rich get richer. Women slave in the maquiladoras, old and broken by the time they're forty; girls are abducted and used by the narcos. It's all the same; all food for the machine that is driving us to our future. And it's only when we recognize the real prison we're in that we can start to find a way out.

Arturo doesn't understand. He doesn't understand half of what Siggy is saying, not in detail, but he doesn't mind. He knows it's important, he thinks he might understand, one day. One thing he does understand now is that Siggy must have changed, somehow, somewhere. That is what he wants to know about the most.

—¿So?—he asks.—¿What happened to you?

Siggy shrugs.

—I wised up. Or I started to. The first thing that dealer made me realize is that I was a migrant too. I came from Austria, but because my parents had money, because we were white, no one gave us a hard time. Almost everyone in America is a migrant, or their families were. Almost everyone. That started me thinking, what that dealer said. I set out on a long journey. I began to understand things. It is a journey I am still making, but at least now I have someone to travel with.

Arturo looks at Carlos. He seems somber, heavy. As if Siggy's mood has infected them all. Arturo sees there are tears collecting in the corners of Carlos's eyes.

—I'm sorry—he says.—Arturo, our friend, I'm sorry. You are in trouble, and I can only cry for us all.

Arturo shakes his head, wondering what is wrong.

—I'm okay—Carlos says.—But our society is so very machista. ¿You know? It can be hard. For people like us, it can be hard. It was hard before I found Siggy. I had no meaning, and you know, man cannot bear a meaningless life. But with Siggy, I found meaning.

Arturo nods, gently. He doesn't know what to say. He doesn't mind about Siggy and Carlos, about their life. He's known them almost all of his short life. He knows some people still give them a hard time, but mostly strangers passing through, not people from Anapra. In Anapra, everyone knows Carlos and his white friend, *the German* from America. Everyone lets them be.

Arturo has a different question for El Alemán.

—¿Siggy? You said you set out on a journey. ¿What did you find?

Siggy shrugs.

—Too many things, I think. I think sometimes it's better to know nothing. Be dumb and happy. ¿Right?

Carlos laughs.

—¡You don't believe that for one minute!

Siggy's head droops, he takes a breath. He seems tired, so tired, and yet he lifts his head once more and looks at Arturo, who frowns. Siggy reaches out his hand and grasps Arturo's forearm tight. Arturo is almost shocked by this gesture, how hard his old friend squeezes his arm. Life comes to Arturo in a moment and everything vibrates around him, as El Alemán looks deep into his eyes, so deep Arturo feels the need to look away, and just as strongly he feels the need to keep looking. The sun has moved farther still. Arturo's face is sliced in two by the soft black shadows of the bars on the window.

—Arturo—Siggy says.—You have to be strong. You will find a way. You will. Carlos and I, we are a long way down the road. You are only just beginning. But you are at the hardest point of all. You are not a kid. You are not a man. You are somewhere in the middle. You are walking over a bridge between the two, and you know how dangerous bridges are. In Juárez we all know how dangerous bridges are. ¿Right? But stay strong, be brave. Your future lies on the other side, and you can make it. Remember this: every man has to find out for himself in what particular fashion he can be saved. I believe that. You just have to find out what it is you're looking for.

And it's just about then, as I talk about these things—as I talk about dishonest trade agreements and corrupt politicians, as I talk about the vested interests of the rich nations, which is to say the rich people who run them, as I talk about life for the poor outside the borders of "civilization," as I talk about shady deals made between dubious organizations—that I realize that people have stopped listening to me. They don't make eye contact with me anymore, they cough quietly and suggest that no one wants to know about these things, and it's just about then that I realize that I am the crazy one, not them. They are sane and sensible and in the right while I am the lunatic, staring at them with mad eyes and thinking furiously to myself that surely we have something better to offer than this: polite embarrassment.

For that, it seems, is all we can manage in the face of these crimes, these breaches of brotherhood, which are the shattering of pledges we made long, long ago around campfires in dark caves, when we swore in our first tongues that we would be as one, and in that way, would prosper.

Polite embarrassment.

Then, I leave the room.

DIOS ESTÁ AQUÍ

As Arturo emerges into the sunlight on the stoop of El Diván, he knows that something has just happened. He has the powerful feeling he has just been given something, though what it is he cannot yet say. He stands for a moment and looks west down Rancho Anapra. From here, he cannot see Mount Cristo Rey and its martyred king. What he sees instead are the people of the colonia, and their dreams. He sees the Adrenaline bike store, the grubby burger joint next to it, and, though their shutters are still rolled down, he can feel the energy inside them, behind them, the energy of people's yearnings and strivings and desires.

A little way down the road, a teenage girl is wheeling a plastic barrel of water she must have bought at the twenty-four-hour kiosk. It's heavy and she's struggling but she's managing. She's going to make it home. A couple of cars come and go, and Arturo catches glimpses of the drivers, feels their needs and their passions. All around him, Anapra lives, despite the horrors, despite the poverty, despite the struggles, and Arturo is sure he has never seen the place in quite this way before. Every color seems just a little brighter, every detail seems just a little sharper, every smell a little stronger. Anapra buzzes into him, and he is sure he has just been given a gift of some kind, he's just not sure what the gift is.

You just have to find out what it is you're looking for, that's what Siggy said. ¿What I'm looking for? Arturo thinks bitterly. ¿Apart from five thousand dollars? He has wasted enough time, and outside El Diván the same world is waiting for Arturo. He knows that he left El Diván as poor as when he went in, and as desperate, and he knows he has only a few hours left in which to save his skin, and Faustino's.

He steps down off the stoop, and is walking away when a voice calls from behind him.

—¡Arturo!

He turns and sees Carlos hurrying out of the door toward him. In his hands is what can only be their five hundred dollars.

—Here—Carlos says.—Take it. Please.

Arturo shakes his head and tries to say no, and that he can't take it, but Carlos will not be persuaded. He reaches out a hand and then, to Arturo's discomfort, taps him right in the middle of the forehead, on the very same spot where Raúl's gun of a finger pointed.

—It's all in here—he says.—With you, it's all in here. So wrapped up in thinking. And I'm telling you to stop thinking. Take the money. Maybe you find nine more people like us today, and you're saved. ¿Right?

It's a ludicrous suggestion, but Arturo cannot win the argument, and in the end Carlos practically shoves the cash into his pocket.

—Listen—he says. He glances over his shoulder at the bar.—There's something else, but I don't think Siggy would want me to tell you. There's someone you should try for the money.

Serpents wind up out of the ground and into Arturo through the soles of his feet. They squirm up his legs and into his body and they whisper to him, *Be afraid, Arturo, be afraid, be afraid*, but what it is he should be afraid of, they will not say. Something just feels wrong, that Carlos would keep something from Siggy, that there is something that Siggy would not want Carlos to tell Arturo. But there is no time to wonder at these things, because Carlos is already whispering hurriedly.

—¿You remember your old teacher? ¿Margarita?

Arturo nods. Yes, of course he remembers her. That year and a half when he went to school, when he and Faustino went to school, they were the best months of his life. And though he has a sudden vision of how Doña Margarita scolded him for smearing paint over Eva's name and her handprint, she was good, she was kind. She even made sure the hungry kids got fed, somehow, when their parents were not able to do it.

—I saw her a while back. You know she moved out of Anapra. ¿Right? Anyway, she's well off now, living in the city. She's the kind of person who would have money and she's the kind of person who would lend it to you.

—¿Really?—asks Artruo.—¿You think so?

Carlos is nodding his head.

—I know so. I have her address. Go there, niño. I know she'll help you. Just don't tell her I sent you, don't tell anyone. Especially not Siggy. ¿Right?

163

He shoves a scrap of paper into Arturo's hands, and Arturo sees a hastily written address.

—Go there, niño. Go there, now.

With that, Carlos steps forward and folds his arms around Arturo briefly. He whispers something in his ear. Then he's gone, leaving his words hanging.

—Siggy is right, you are on the bridge. Be careful.

Arturo looks at the address; it's somewhere in the area called Versalles. He's never been there, but he knows it's upmarket. Margarita must have made good somehow, really good.

Yet he hesitates. He used to see her all the time, in the streets of Anapra, always with kids around her, none of them her own. He hasn't seen her in a couple of years, and now he knows why: she moved somewhere better, and he cannot blame her for that.

He's just looking at the address again when he sees the Five coming, the bus heading into the city. He fishes in his pocket and sees he has enough pesos left from what Faustino gave him. Enough for a ride into town. So he knows that Santa Muerte has not left him altogether, perhaps. Perhaps she is angry with him and testing him again, but has not abandoned him completely. So he runs across the street in time to flag the bus to a stop. Moments later, he's riding into Juárez for the second time in twenty-four hours.

- *NAFTA: the North American Free Trade Agreement. A minor footnote in the American presidential election of 1992, barely discussed or debated.*

- *NAFTA: part of what James Morgan of the* Financial Times *described as the "new imperial age," the "de facto world government": the International Monetary Fund, the World Bank, the Group of Seven nations, and other such organizations.*

- *One notable feature of such organizations is their immunity to popular influence; to give one example, various groups wishing to comment on the NAFTA treaty were given less than a day to read it and submit their thoughts on a document that runs to several hundred pages.*

- *"Free trade" is a somewhat misleading term; many of the rules in NAFTA are aimed at making trade more advantageous for American companies; it is due to NAFTA that the maquiladoras of Mexico are able to flourish.*

- *In 1998 the US International Trade Commission estimated that American companies stood to gain $61 billion a year from developing nations because of such schemes.*

FIVE IS THE BRIDGE

The ride is slow and hot. The morning is wearing on and the bus stops frequently as more and more people climb aboard, heading into the city. Arturo stares out of the window, speaking to no one, trying to make eye contact as little as possible. He rode the same way last night, with Faustino, then he curses himself; he should have left a message with Carlos, just in case Faustino comes by. He hopes his four aces are still tucked into the doorframe; he hopes they can still be read.

At the church of San Lorenzo, Arturo gets off the bus. This is Juárez at its finest. This is not a city that reeks of violent death, of mutilated cadavers in the dust that blows in from the desert. Here are expensive stores; smart streets filled with cars that do not look as though they are about to drop dead.

He walks down the sidewalk beside a six-lane highway that carves through the heart of the city. Here are more totems: a giant Pemex station, then later a Shell station. Burger King. And the only sign that perhaps everything is not totally right with the world is the line of people, a block long. Arturo sees what they're queuing for: a bank. They're lining up to use the ATM. Something wrong maybe, some financial scare, perhaps the people want their money out before it's gone forever.

He walks on.

It's still a way to Versalles and he has never been there before. He stops people a couple of times, gets directions, and heads on, and then he's on Margarita's street: Calle Valle de los Olivos.

It's a nice street. Most of the houses have two stories. Many are set back from the road, behind tall gates with spikes on the top, but the gates are new and the houses are freshly painted and everywhere are the signs of money: kids' bikes propped by the front door, nice plants in pots standing to the side. Good cars parked outside, fancy ones even.

Arturo checks the address one more time: number five.

Five, again. He remembers the fives he was dealt last night, playing calavera. Five is the turning point, five is the only moment when you have to make a call, one way or the other. Five is the bridge, and he's on the bridge now.

He looks at the house; it's not finished; parts of it are unpainted concrete and bare brick, but it's going to be beautiful. It's two floors and it's not just something thrown up as fast and cheaply as possible. It has been thought about, it has been designed. Through the gates, Arturo sees that five little steps twist up from ground level in a quarter spiral to the door. Just to the left of that is an open balcony with large glass windows, and yes, there are shutters that can be brought down, but no bars. There's a carport to one side, and there's a brand-new gold-colored Jeep lurking in the shadows there.

He tries the gate. It's locked, of course, but he sees there is an intercom in the pillar beside it. Without thinking any further, he tries the buzzer.

Nothing.

He tries it again, and then he hears dogs barking inside, at least two dogs. He's about to walk away when the intercom hisses.

It's a woman's voice; it could be her, it's hard to tell.

—¿Hola?

—¿Margarita?

—Yes—says the voice.—¿Who is it?

—Arturo.

—¿Arturo who?

Arturo isn't surprised. It's been a couple of years. At least.

—Arturo Silva.

There is a long pause. A very long pause. The intercom has gone silent. Arturo turns away; she's given him as clear an answer as any she could have spoken. She wants nothing to do with him and cannot even be bothered to tell him so. But the intercom hisses again.

—Come in—the voice says, and the gate buzzes and Arturo presses himself against it quickly before she changes her mind.

The door opens before Arturo is even halfway across the yard.

She stands there, waiting for him. She is looking at Arturo strangely. He cannot read the mixture of thoughts that are pouring from her head, but he can tell one thing: she looks at him as if she's looking at a ghost. But there are other things too, other, darker things.

She looks more or less the same; a little older, a little plumper, perhaps. Her eyes are tired but they still smile at him as she suddenly rushes forward and throws her arms around him.

—¡Arturo! ¡Dios mío!

She steps back, staring at him, shaking her head.

—You scared me—she says next, and Arturo feels the serpents crawling into him again, ancient serpents that know more than we do.

—¿Scared you? ¿Why?

Margarita shakes her head, as if disbelieving something.

—Because I thought you were dead, Arturo. I thought you were dead.

From nowhere, Arturo laughs. He cannot help himself.

—¡But here I am!—he says.—¡Here I am! Alive.

He cannot bring himself to say *alive and well*, but the bad joke that Margarita thought he was dead is too much for him to ignore. And he isn't dead yet, not yet.

—So I see—says Margarita and then Arturo sees the darker things surfacing again. Anger is one of them.

—I don't understand—he says.—¿Why did you think I was dead?

—Because he told me you were, of course—she says, and her face has darkened with that anger.

—¿He?—Arturo asks.—¿Who's he?

Now it's Margarita who looks confused.

—¡My God!—she says.—¿Who else? Your father, of course. ¿You've come to see him? ¿Right?

Then something moves in the doorway over Margarita's shoulder, and Arturo looks there, and sees a man staring at him, and yes, it is his father.

THE PRIMAL KILLING

Now the world has erupted and bends and breaks and folds in on itself.
Now the ancient gods crawl out from under rocks where they have
lurked for centuries. Now they slide into the October sunlight, their
claws clacking and their tongues lolling in expectation, in anticipa-
tion of blood, primal blood. It is all Arturo can do not to be sucked
down into the maw of the earth, right here and now. Sucked down
into deep and terrifying regions of the underworld, there to be
destroyed.

Arturo stares and his father stares back and Arturo knows he
has to fight the urge in him, the urge to run, because there is nothing he wants to do more right now than that; run, just pound his
way out of the city and into the desert and lie in the dust and die,
to be consumed by dogs. He fights that desire, because if he runs,
he will never know. He will never find out anything. And he won't
know what is happening here in this house, where he has found
his old teacher with his father.

Margarita is looking between the two of them. Arturo sees there is anger inside her, barely concealed, and yet he also sees that she is doing her best to withhold her anger. He knows without question that she is doing it for his sake.

She takes a step toward the doorway, turns back to Arturo.

—I think you'd better come in—she says.

Arturo does not want to, because there is his father, blocking the way. He wants to run, but then he sees his father run a hand backward over his hair and sigh and turn aside, allowing the way in.

Arturo looks at Margarita, who nods.

It's dark inside the house. The sunlight seems to barely penetrate, and where Arturo's father stands in the hall he is just a hunched silhouette, blocking the path inside. But he moves, goes farther in, and Arturo sees he has no choice but to follow.

Somehow, Arturo finds himself sitting on a leather sofa, a real leather sofa, in their living room. It's almost impossible for him to understand that this all belongs to his father. The room is full of expensive things: a knife-thin TV, a laptop, art. Art, thinks Arturo. He has enough money to spend on pictures for the walls, and trinkets to put on the shelf. His father sits opposite him, his back to a tall window. Margarita stands to the side, between them, her arms folded, her mouth shut tight.

It is Arturo who speaks first.

—¿How long?—he asks.—¿How long has this been going on?

He waves a hand from Margarita to his father.

His father says nothing. He stares at a point on the top of the low table that lies between them, unblinking.

—A couple of years—Margarita says. She looks at the floor, and then turns her head sideways.

—Roberto told me you were dead—she adds, and her voice is cold and sharp.

Arturo stares at his father.

—¿You told her I was dead?

Roberto Silva lifts his head, stabs a forefinger toward his son.

—You are dead. I told you that. ¿Or have you forgotten?

Margarita is pacing up and down now. Arturo sees her hold her hand to her mouth.

—¿You know what happened?—he asks her.—¿Right?

She stops walking and stares at Arturo.

—I see—says Arturo.—He didn't tell you.

He stares at his father as he speaks.

—He didn't tell you how he nearly killed me. He didn't tell you how he got so drunk, night after night. He didn't tell you that he beat me. He didn't tell you how he burned our crappy place to the ground one night with me inside.

—¡I didn't know you were inside!—Roberto snaps, irritated. But not angry, it seems, not sorry.

—¡Yes, you did! And if you didn't, it was only because you were off your head with pulque.

Margarita has stopped pacing up and down and is staring at Roberto.

—And you told me he was dead. When we met, when we got together, you told me he was dead. ¿How many more lies have you told me?

—He is dead—Arturo's father says.—He is dead to me. He knew that. There was no reason to tell you differently.

—¿What?—Margarita shouts.—¿What are you talking about?

Roberto does not answer. He glares at Arturo, as if challenging him.

Arturo knows that look, and that he was afraid of it once. He is not afraid of it anymore. He holds his father's stare as he explains to Margarita.

—The day after the fire. The neighbors actually called the police. And it must have been a quiet day because they even came to see what had happened. And my father told me I had to tell them it was an accident, that the fire was an accident.

—¿It wasn't?—asks Margarita and her voice is trembling and her hand is halfway to her mouth again.

—You tell us, Father—says Arturo.—You were drunk and I was asleep and you poured gasoline on the outside of the shack and set it alight. ¿Was that an accident?

Arturo tries to fight the memories of that night: the flames in the dark, the shouting and his childish fear that the burning jacal was going to set the whole world on fire; that the world would burn before the flames died out. And none of that as bad as what he was most afraid of, the man sitting in front of him now.

Roberto says nothing. Margarita is motionless, rigid with fear and horror and betrayal.

—And then—Arturo says—I told the police what had happened, and they put him in jail. For a night. He tried to kill me and they put him in jail for a night. Then he came back to Anapra and found me and beat me so badly I thought I would never walk again. He told me I was dead, and left me.

Roberto Silva continues to glare at his son. Margarita barely breathes. Only Arturo finds that he is calm, that a tranquil emptiness has entered him and that this emptiness is holding him up, supporting him.

—¿When was this?—Margarita asks.—¿After you stopped coming to school?

—A year or so—Arturo says.—I was just thirteen.

Margarita is shaking her head.

—¿And you didn't know about this? ¿You didn't know about us, I mean?

Arturo doesn't answer.

Then Margarita says—Carlos. How you found us. ¿Right?

And Arturo doesn't answer that either, and then Margarita turns away from them both, facing the wall. No one moves. There is no sound, there is just pain hanging in the room, filling it with an atmosphere of poison.

From nowhere Margarita picks a thin glass vase off the shelf and whirls, flinging it at Roberto. He throws his arms up to protect himself and the glass shatters all over him in hundreds of small pieces, and with it, the atmosphere is shattered. Margarita unleashes her anger upon him, cursing him, berating him, and she is crying too and she only stops when another sound of crying comes to them.

From upstairs, the cries of a baby drift down, and with that, Margarita hurls one last tirade of her anger at Roberto, and then hurries away to soothe the child.

—¿You're a father? ¿Again?—Arturo asks, once she's gone.

Roberto barely moves. Pieces of glass lie in his lap, even in his hair. As always, Arturo notices, he seems untouched, while others around him suffer. More than that, Arturo hates the way he cannot, even now, be normal. Cannot be a normal father to a normal son. He just sits, motionless like the statue of a god, an ignorant, tribal god.

—¿Still drinking?—Arturo asks, and hates himself for playing these games, for being so easily cheap as to try to find cheap, easy ways of hurting his father, of getting some reaction out of him, anything, anything at all, even anger. But his father just sits there.

Arturo waves a hand to indicate the room they're sitting in, the house.

—So it turned out all right for you, then.

Roberto scratches behind his ear, slowly, staring at Arturo.

—¿What do you want, Arturo? ¿Why did you come here?

—I came to see Margarita—he says.—I thought she could . . . And instead I find you.

From upstairs, the sound of the baby crying. There's also the sound of Margarita singing and that is almost too much for Arturo to bear because it is the same song she used to sing to the little kids at school when they were upset. It is one memory too much for Arturo. Those days, when he went to school and Faustino and Eva and he were just kids and his father didn't drink too much and his mother, his mother was still . . .

—She is too good for you—Arturo says, and for a second, Arturo *is* suddenly afraid as he thinks his father is going to leap across the table and throttle him to death.

Instead, Roberto takes a long breath and runs a hand over his hair.

—¿So? ¿Why did you come to see Margarita? ¿What could she possibly help you with?

¿Why not just say it? Arturo thinks. ¿Why not just say it? There is no reason not to.

—I need money. I need a lot of money, and I came to borrow it from her. But now I see that it's your money I've come to borrow.

For the first time, Arturo gets some kind of reaction out of his father: surprise.

—You want to borrow money. From me.

—That's right. Cabrón.

Arturo knows Margarita guessed correctly; that Carlos must have sent him here, and Arturo also guesses that Carlos knew that his father was here. That was what Siggy wanted to be kept secret, and there, thinks Arturo, is the difference between them, because Carlos believes that, despite everything, Roberto will help his son. Whereas Siggy believes that he will do no such thing and it will only bring more pain and more anguish. Arturo knows all that, in an instant, and he supposes that he is about to find out which of them is right.

He also knows that he is not going to beg, he is not going to beg. But he has to do this, he has to say it, he must, for his own sake, and for Faustino's and also, therefore, for Eva, for the baby. If the baby is to have a father, Arturo needs to get this money. So he asks for it.

—I came to borrow money. I thought I was asking Margarita, but now I see I have come to ask you. I need five thousand dollars. And I need them right now. And in fact, I don't want to borrow it, I want you to give it to me.

Roberto stares at him, his face still impassive.

—¿Why should I do that?

177

—I'm in trouble. I got into some trouble with some narcos and I owe them five thousand. By tonight.

—Five thousand dollars is a lot of money.

Arturo hates him. He hates him for playing games, for not being a normal father to a normal son. He gave up years ago wondering why his father hates him so much, a question he asked himself a million times, but one that he knows his father never asked himself. Which was, Arturo decided in the end, the answer in itself. Why does his father hate him? He just does. But then Arturo thinks about Eva and the baby, and he knows what it is to have no father and so he clenches his teeth and asks again.

—I need it. ¿Will you give it to me, or not?

Just tell me, chingada, Arturo thinks. Just damn well tell me.

—That's a lot of money.

Arturo does not answer. He waits, hoping that, once his father has played his games, he will put his hand in his pocket and give him the cash.

—You know—Roberto says—I ought to thank you. For all this, I mean.

—¿Why?

—You could have got me killed, getting me sent to the cells that night. You have no idea what it's like in there. No idea. I hated you for that.

—¿Yeah?—says Arturo scathingly.

—Yeah. There was a fight in the cell next to me; this big guy smashed some poor pendejo to nothing. Broke his head open on the floor, and the cops . . . they did nothing. No, that's not true. They stood and laughed. Then they placed bets on how far the blood would run across the floor.

Arturo tries to show no emotion, and yet, despite everything, despite himself, despite all the luxury around him, he feels sorry. He feels sorry for his father, and scared for him, his father of years ago, stuck in a jail cell overnight, because of him. No, he tells himself. No. *He* did it. *He* burned that shack down and I was scared. I was just a kid and I was really, really scared.

Arturo shakes his head.

—¿So why should you be thanking me?

—Because I met a guy that night; he gave me his phone number. A while later, I looked him up. He gave me a job. And now, as you see, life is good.

Roberto smiles.

There's a shudder, a giant shuddering as the earth stumbles once more. It trips over its own revolutions, just for a split second, a vast heart skipping a beat, and Arturo reels and feels the dangers rising out of the cleft in the ground that has been steadily opening beneath him. Things crawl up his legs, worming through his skin like maggots and into his poor heart and then he hears himself asking his father a question.

—¿What job?

His father waves a hand.

—I'm a driver. It's a simple job.

His father is still smiling and the smile sends the maggots into a frenzy and they eat Arturo's heart from the inside out as Arturo knows that something is wrong, something is wrong, something is desperately wrong. Then his father stands and starts to slowly unbutton his shirt, button by button, and he stands and as fragments of glass tumble to the floor he shows Arturo what lies there.

Inked across his body is a vast tattoo; in the center there is a god-king, bare-chested, with a headdress of the feathers of the sacred quetzal. His arms are outstretched in a gesture of power. Beside him stand warriors and warrior women, fierce, noble. But this is nothing. What Arturo sees above this ridiculous pomposity is what draws his gaze, what has transfixed him.

The number 21. Written bold and large, dominating the scene below. The number 21, and Arturo knows that the 2 means B and the 1 means A. And BA means Barrio Azteca, and that is who his father is driving for, for one of the most powerful pandillas, or maybe even for the cartel itself, and that is where the money has come from that is building this fancy house in which he and Margarita live with their child.

Margarita has returned from upstairs. She's standing on the bottom step, the sleeping baby in her arms.

—She's asleep now—Margarita says quietly.—So no more shouting. ¿Right?

Her anger has gone. She stands on the step, gently rocking the baby on her hip, gently rocking her to keep her asleep, Arturo's half-sister.

—¿What did you come for?—Margarita asks Arturo.

—He came for money—Roberto says, before Arturo can answer.

—So give him money—Margarita says.

Arturo's father looks him in the eye, as he says—No.

Arturo does not move.

He does not beg, he does not shout. He nods at Margarita, and for a moment thinks about going over to see his sister.

He doesn't.

He looks at his father, hating him, and hating himself for still caring. He thinks of all the things that he could say to hurt him.

He says none of them.

He leaves.

¿But what other reaction is there to the world than this? Anger. Anger at the way the world has been divided. In Central America, in Asia, in Africa, in the Middle East, even in Europe, people are leaving their homes to find something better. ¡Believe me, this is no easy step to take! To leave everything you know and set off into the blue . . .

In the past, there would have been revolutions. ¡In France, in Russia, right here in Mexico, when people found themselves with unbearable lives, they rose up! ¡Faced with the intolerable, they overthrew their oppressors! Now, the oppressors are not emperors; they are transnational corporations that are so powerful that even nations cannot control them. They span borders, they operate in many countries and it is hard to know who they are and what they do. And so the people do not know who to rebel against. So there are no revolutions; instead, people walk. Or they get on a boat, or they climb on a freight train. ¿Right? They go to another country looking for work, for a better life, for a life away from these wars and persecution.

And they end up in the rich countries, and you know what people there say . . . ¡Migrants! ¡Illegal aliens! But everyone is a migrant, everyone, outside of the African cradle. It's just a question of how far back in time you care to look . . .

SANTA MUERTE

There were times, and they were always nighttimes, when Arturo dreamed of killing his father. His father might be out at El Diván, making himself more unpopular. Or he might have found some mescal to bring home to their shack. Either way, he would become the subject of young Arturo's fantasies. He never really saw how he did it, in those dreams, he would just linger over the thought that he had killed this hideous monster, this drunken beast. That he had freed himself from the beatings and the sadness and the fear, but if he ever got as far as picturing himself holding a knife, or shooting his father with some imaginary weapon, the fantasy would dissolve. Once the night was past, Arturo would always find himself dangling around his hungover father, getting him coffee, fixing him eggs if they had any. His father might even seem guilty sometimes, though he would never apologize, and would avoid looking at Arturo's bruises. And Arturo would feel guilty too, and think to himself, over and over, I don't want you dead, I don't want you dead, I don't really want you dead.

Father killed Son. Or maybe Son killed Father. Neither actually happened, but both came close; an action left undone, a deed conceived but never completed.

The fire, however, was a deed that *had* happened, and afterward they never saw each other again, save once, when Arturo was crossing Rancho Anapra one day, and saw his father in the distance, looking as old, drunk, and mean as he had ever been, and where he was living and what he was doing was something Arturo forced himself to stop thinking about.

Things change, Arturo knows. Things change, things can always change, but he still cannot believe that his father works for the Barrio Azteca, or that he got himself together, or that he hooked up with Margarita. That she fell for his mierda. That they have a baby daughter. And what was in Margarita's eyes? What was it, aside from the anger, there was something else dark . . .

He wanders, without purpose, without further thought, away from the house, back the way he came. As he reaches the highway and the first of the gas stations he sees a large sign that alternates between displaying the temperature and the time.

It's well after two o'clock. He knows he is as good as finished, but he walks on anyway. It doesn't matter where he goes, she will find him anyway, though for now, she seems to have truly abandoned him.

It's as he's coming back past the bank that an image presents itself to him. The line is still there, but it's shorter now. People stand, waiting, chatting, grumbling patiently, and Arturo sees that they have been standing there so long that they have become oblivious to the world around them. Occasionally someone at the head of the line finishes at the ATM, and the line shuffles forward a little, an almost totally unconscious act.

As he looks at the line shuffle, he sees a young woman at the head of the line. The image rises up in Arturo's head and without thinking further, he acts on it. He's never had money, but he's heard enough to know that if people are scared about their savings, if they think the bank is going under, they will take out as much as they are allowed from the machine. From across the parking lot of the bank, under the shade of a small tree, Arturo watches as the woman completes three separate transactions, putting a card into the machine three times, while behind people grumble at her for taking so long. She studiously ignores them, and doesn't move away until she has taken the last stack of money from the ATM and put it in her purse.

She sets off, briskly, and walks right past Arturo. She doesn't see him. She has car keys out but she's leaving the bank parking lot behind. It's obvious why: it's full, stuffed with all the cars of people waiting in line. But next door are two office blocks, with their own parking spaces. It's Saturday; they're unused, apart from by the handful of people unable to find a space outside the bank.

Arturo turns and slowly follows the woman, putting his hand in his pocket to check that Catrina is still there. She is.

The woman holds her arm out and the lights on a white Mitsubishi all flash, twice. It's just steps away. Arturo takes a look around and then runs.

In a moment he has her arm behind her back and the knife in front of her face, and he's pushing her down the alley between the two office blocks.

He's lucky. She's too afraid, or too smart, to scream, to make trouble. Maybe something like this has even happened to her before, because she knows the routine.

—¡Okay, okay!—she's saying.—¡Take the money, take it! ¡Leave me alone and take it!

Arturo twists her around so she faces him, but keeps the knife out toward her. He has her backed into the shadow of the side door to one of the offices. It's Saturday, they're closed, no lights inside, just darkness.

He doesn't look at the young woman. He looks at her hands, holding her bag, and he waves the knife to get her to hurry. He knows it will not do to look at her, and he tries hard, but he cannot help it.

She's scared, he can see. She might know the routine but she's shaking so badly that she can't open her purse to get at the money.

—I'm sorry—she stammers.—I'm sorry.

Arturo doesn't want to look at her, but he does. She's not much older than he is. She has nice clothes, some simple jewelry. She's never gone hungry in her life, that's clear, but Arturo looks at her and knows she's not a bad person.

But he needs the money and he waves the knife and points at her bag and cannot bring himself to speak and instead he looks just behind her.

There, in the reflection made by the tinted black door to the offices, he sees himself. He sees the back of the girl, fumbling. She fumbles so badly she spills the entire contents of her bag over the ground and she doesn't even seem to remember that she's being held at knifepoint because she stoops and starts picking everything up.

Arturo looks at himself. He had no idea he was so thin, he had no idea he looked so rough. He sees a stupid boy holding a knife, and then he sees what's behind him. He's holding Catrina, but behind them is a woman much more powerful, much more deadly. Why he hadn't seen her before, he doesn't know, but she's there as large as death: Santa Muerte.

She stands completely still. She waits, behind Arturo, her eyes boring into him, her arms outstretched, and in one hand she holds her scythe and in the other she holds the world. She waits, and Arturo watches himself, and now he sees the girl has stood up again and is holding out a bundle of money toward him. He has no idea how much it is. It's not even dollars. It's pesos. But he doesn't care anymore.

—I'm sorry—the girl says, still holding the money, and then the look on her face starts to change.

Slowly, carefully, she puts the money back in her purse, and Arturo watches it all happening and there is Santa Muerte, right behind him. He lets his arm drop. He folds the knife and puts it back in his pocket.

He cannot look at the girl as he says—Forgive me.

He nods toward the parking lot.

—Go on.

The girl doesn't understand why this is happening, but she sees her chance, and half walks, half runs away, looking back at Arturo every other step, checking she's not being followed.

She isn't.

Arturo doesn't see her anymore. He looks at himself in the glass, and knows he has to turn around to look at Santa Muerte directly.

It takes a massive effort of will. It's hard, because tendrils have snaked out of the ground and are twining around his legs, holding him where he is, but he knows he has to face her, and so he wrenches his legs free and makes a half turn, and even as he does so and plants his feet on the ground again, the tendrils start to reattach themselves, twisting around and into him. They are the past, of past history, of lies made in the past, they are the tendrils of promises made and broken, come to seek the revenge they crave.

The White Girl, meanwhile, stares at him, Arturo. It's impossible to read her bone face for emotion. It could be anything. It could be hate, it could be kindness. It could be empathy, it could be anger. It could be mocking laughter that pours from her silent face, her gaping mouth.

Whoever made her has done a very good job. She's three meters high, maybe more, and covers half the side of the ground floor of the other office block. She's mostly black and white, just a touch of color here and there, sprayed onto the brick wall with auto paint. The scythe is gold, the world in her hands is a dying green, not the green of fertile growth but the green of decay, of putrefaction.

¿What have I done? thinks Arturo. ¿What have I lost?

He stares at Santa Muerte, she stares back. As before, she wins. She always wins, and Arturo lets his gaze drop, and knows that he is done. That he has failed. That there is nothing else to do but to go back to Isla de Sacrificios, and wait. It's over.

Something disturbs him, a noise to his right. He looks up and sees four people by a car. The car is a police car, and three of the people are policemen, and the fourth is the young woman he just tried to rob. She's pointing at him, and the cops see that he has spotted them, and they shout.

—¡Hey!

—¡Stop!

Arturo sees them pull their guns from the holsters, and he turns away.

At the far end of the alley between the office blocks is a low wire fence. Beyond it is waste ground, beyond that, strip malls and fast food joints.

He glances at the ground, expecting to find the tendrils holding him fast, but, with surprise, sees he is free, and sprints for the fence.

He only saw the cops for a second but he spotted that at least two of them are out of shape. They cannot bring their car this way; he need only be fast enough to get away and across the waste ground.

This is the thought in his head as he throws himself at the low chain-link fence, grabbing its rusty wires with his hands and vaulting his legs up and over it. He lands in a messy sprawl, and a shot whistles past his head.

The cops are shouting and he can hear running behind him, but he doesn't stop to think. He's up on his feet and, ignoring the pain in one ankle, he sprints across the patch of ground, with his head back and his arms clawing for air.

Another shot, and this time he only hears the bang of the gun, and guesses he is putting distance between them. Ahead, he sees the malls. They're full of people. They won't shoot again, not with these people, and he even allows himself to turn and sees the first of the cops struggling over the fence, a hundred meters away now, maybe more.

Arturo ducks and weaves his way through the crowds, losing himself, losing himself, though he doesn't really need to bother.

In truth, he is already lost.

STATELESS

Arturo slows to a walk, settles down, trying to merge into the crowd, trying to become one of them but never really settling. He is not them. As much as he tries and as much as he might like to be, he is not one of them. They are dressed better than him, they wash in fresh water every day, they have money. Arturo stands apart.

He thinks about running. Not running from these overfed cops, not running home. He thinks about running away, completely, and not for the first time. Brief but elaborate fantasies burst through his mind, fantasies in which he is lucky and finds work or steals a fortune or is taken in by kindly people and is happy. Fantasies like these, and more. He creates every one, and then destroys it. He sees El Carnero holding the phone up to his face, taking his picture. In minutes Arturo's face can be sent to every pandilla sympathetic to the cartel and he would be walking a nightmare of a deathful expectation. He could run, yes, he could run, but where? How far would he get? What would he live on?

Arturo walks on down the strip mall, clinging to the shop

windows, away from the street. He knows the cops will not follow him now. If they don't chase you after the first block, they don't chase you, but he's careful, he's safe, that's what has kept him alive for this long, and now he's no less cautious. He glances at people as they slide by him, all hurrying; in fact, Arturo suddenly sees, all *running*. Whether they're walking or hurrying or ambling or whatever it is, they're all running, running, *running*.

He wonders what it is they're running from. Perhaps it's something they're running *to*, but then, as he watches, they start to wind down, like a clockwork mechanism grinding to a halt, step by step, slowing to a stop. Arturo stops still, watching them wide-eyed, wondering what is happening as they all become motionless around him, frozen in time, still.

He blinks. He stares. He becomes afraid he is paralyzed too and jerks his hand to show himself he can move. Seeing that he can, he walks. Since they are stopped in time, motionless, he is able to come right up to people and stare at them, gaze at them for as long as he likes.

He approaches a couple, arm in arm. They are caught in the moment of turning to each other and smiling, and Arturo feels his heart slide as he looks at them, but then, as he looks closer, he sees something else. There is something behind the woman's smile, and the man's too. He sees the happiness they have in being together, in looking at each other, but underneath he sees something else, a lurking and nameless thing, a terror.

Dismayed, Arturo spins around and turns to an old man behind him. He looks into the man's face, deeply, looking right into his eyes, more closely than anyone has done in decades. The man's face is impassive, but Arturo sees through his eyes and feels his soul twisting.

¿With what? thinks Arturo. ¿What is it? ¿Pain, fear? ¿Loneliness? What does Arturo see, what does he feel?

He is grasping for it, flailing, reaching as he turns and looks about him, and on all sides, with everyone he approaches, it's the same thing.

Arturo reels backward, made dizzy by this thing he cannot name, staggering from host to host and finding only the same thing inside. The same appalling truth, the same abysmal horror and Arturo knows that this horror is only unnameable for the moment. That it will burst forth, sooner or later, erupt across the stage of the mind, the stage of the world and be known for what it is, and then people will sink to their knees and weep with understanding. They will tilt their heads back, turn their faces to the heavens, and beg and pray, and the heavens will answer with nothing but silence, for all the gods will have vanished.

Arturo stares into the soul of a young woman, a girl about his own age, transfixed by the dawning horror, on the cusp of understanding. Something distracts him. The girl has her hand lifted and is brushing her hair aside from her face. Her wrist bears an expensive watch, and Arturo is distracted by it.

Because time does not move, the hands on the watch do not move, not even the second hand, but Arturo reads the time. It is just after three. He told Faustino to meet him at five, back in Anapra. Then, the moment is broken.

There's a shout, the second hand of the watch gives out a staggering *tick* and Arturo turns his head away from the girl and sees the cops at the end of the street. He was wrong, they did follow him. With that shout, everyone starts moving around him again, just as before, like normal, and Arturo looks at his legs and his feet and the ground beneath them, and sees they are free. With that, he runs.

He runs home, across the city, sprinting hard, dodging and weaving, jumping on a bus to take him back to Anapra. He has failed to find five thousand dollars, he failed to find the four he needs to save his own skin, failed to find the one that Faustino needs. He has the five hundred from Siggy and Carlos, and that is not enough to save either of them. But maybe Faustino has had better luck, maybe he has come up with something. Maybe there is still a way out, for both of them. Or maybe not for both of them, and with that, a new thought enters Arturo's head, something remarkable, one that takes root and begins to spread rapidly through his mind. He hurries up from Rancho Anapra to his place, praying that all will be well, praying that Faustino will be there. He isn't.

When he gets to his shack he sees three of the aces still stuck in the doorframe. The fourth is on the ground outside. Arturo pushes his way inside, and there he finds a note from Faustino, written in ballpoint on the opened-out interior of a discarded cigarette pack.

¿Where are you? You have to have the money.
Meet me at mine at 12. F

Arturo stares at the note.

Faustino was here. He was here some time before twelve; they must have both been in Anapra at the same time and missed each other. And when Arturo didn't show up in Calle Libertad at twelve, what did Faustino think then? Will he still come back at five, as Arturo told him to?

There is no way to know, no other way to find out, than to wait.

Arturo is exhausted. He lies down on his bed, and then, feeling in his pocket, discovers that Catrina is missing. The knife must have fallen from his pocket somewhere, when he was running from the cops, leaping over that fence, and he knows that he has lost the best thing he owned.

He is not aware of it yet, but he will receive three visitors this evening. The order in which they come will determine his fate. In the meantime, something he has been trying to ignore rises up in him, something he knows he can no longer avoid, *someone* he has to think about, finally.

So while Arturo waits for Faustino, he spends his time thinking about another person altogether: Eva.

One—Climate change is now indisputably recognized to be the result of global industrialization.

Two—The greatest single impact of climate change will be on human migration, with millions of people displaced by drought, shoreline erosion, coastal flooding, and agricultural disruption.

Three—The impact of climate change is anticipated to displace up to 250 million people worldwide by 2050.

Four—Speaking at the United Nations conference on climate change in Paris, French president Francois Hollande said: "Never have the stakes been so high, because this is about the future of the planet, the future of life."

Five—"This is the turning point."

EVA

Arturo knows most of Eva's story. The rest he can guess. Hers is like so many others. He knows those lives, they all know them.

Like Arturo, Eva was born in Juárez. Not in Anapra, though, but in the Colonia Franja Sara Lugo, also right by the border, east a little way. It lies just across the river from Smeltertown, the Asarco plant, a place that is now empty, shut down after it was finally proved the company used it to illegally dispose of hazardous waste. They demolished the towering smokestacks a couple of years back, but by then decades of damage had been done.

Eva's mother remembers those days bitterly, and will tell anyone who cares to listen as well as those who don't. Arturo knows the stories she used to tell, stories about the wind. They hated the north wind more than anything, for it was on those days that the Asarco plant would crank up production, and the smokestack would pour sulfur dioxide and heavy metals directly into Mexico, directly into the colonias south of the border.

—They could pollute us as much as they wanted—Eva's mother

would say.—And because it was coming from another country, no one could stop them. ¿What could we do? We just breathed it all in.

And then Eva's mother will tell anyone who's listening and anyone who's not about the two stillbirths she had before she had Eva, and, unspoken, dare anyone to deny that the deformed things that came out of her womb did not have anything to do with Smeltertown.

Eva was lucky. She survived nine months inside her mother. Just before the new millennium was born, Eva was born into a colonia just as poor as Anapra, where she and her mother would move later, when Eva's father died. She was five at the time, and doesn't really remember him. She remembers the Asarco smokestacks, though production had been stopped by then and the monstrous chimneys stood silent, monuments to foregoing greed. She remembers playing with other kids on the waste ground right by the river. There were two white shacks, built of bricks, and a smaller one, unpainted. She and the other kids would climb on them and, when they were too tired to run and play anymore, sit on the roofs and make up stories about the sleeping giants who lived in the now silent smelting plant across the river.

When her father died, they would have been homeless, but they moved to Anapra where they lived with Eva's mother's brothers and their families. Eva's two uncles had been building a house of sorts out here to the northwest of the city where land was free if you could grab it and keep it. Eva's mother got a job in the Electrolux factory, then took a second shift, this one in the Boeing plant. She aged rapidly, she barely saw her daughter, but they had enough money to survive. Eva began going to school, and it was there, a few years later, that she met Arturo and Faustino: the brothers who were not, she eventually learned, actually brothers.

Arturo and Faustino were already friends, of course. One day, not long after they had begun going to the school, some other kid was teasing Faustino, taunting him about his foot. The kid hobbled around the yard outside the classroom, pointing at Faustino and pulling dumb faces, making some of the other kids laugh. Eva didn't laugh. She walked right up to the kid, who wasn't so big really, and stamped on his foot so hard they said she'd broken his toes. She got in trouble, but after that no one teased Faustino about his foot again. Faustino was embarrassed that a girl had saved him from the bully, but Arturo told him he should say thank you, so he did.

She just shrugged.

—It's not right—she said.—To make fun of people.

Arturo and Faustino nodded, seriously.

And that was that.

Why the three of them became such close friends, no one really knew, but it was as if the brothers who were not brothers wanted a sister, even though Eva was not their sister.

They did everything together. For the year and a half that Arturo and Faustino were at school they learned together. Out of school they played together. They laughed and laughed and ran and cried, and they fought, like the time with the handprints and the paint on the school wall when Margarita got so mad at them. Though they were close, the three of them, there was something strange about the way they were; something they felt but were too young to know.

There were three of them, and three points should form a triangle, but Arturo and Faustino and Eva did not. They were a line, and on one end was Arturo and on the other end was Eva, while Faustino was in the middle. He was the one who made it all work, he was the bridge between Arturo and Eva, stopped them from squabbling, made them all happy. He would appease Eva's moods, he would cheer Arturo up from the gloom he sometimes sank into, and they grew up that way, not seeing that things were changing, that they were changing, and that the distance Faustino had to travel back and forth between Eva and Arturo was now greater than ever.

One day, Arturo thinks as he lies on his bunk in his shack on the Isla de Sacrificios, one day, the line that had been stretching and stretching just snapped. They'd probably stopped being friends months before, they just didn't know it. They had all grown, and when you grow you can either grow together, or grow apart. They would bicker with each other, all three of them; they'd stopped having fun, and the time had to come eventually when one of them would realize it. That was the day that Faustino left, took Eva, and went to live with her mother, who was by then living in Chaveña.

Arturo didn't see them again. That was a year ago, he calculates, almost a year ago, and until they showed up in Faustino's car, he hadn't seen them in all that time.

Arturo's breathing slows.

He feels he is barely here in the world as he admits to himself: Well, that's not exactly true. ¿Is it?

He might not have seen Faustino for almost a year, but he had seen Eva. Just once. And it is this once that is troubling him. With everything that has happened, he hasn't had time to think when it was that he saw Eva. That's what he tells himself, but he knows that's a lie too. He thinks of Siggy. *The first person a liar lies to is himself.* He has had more than enough time to work out when it was that he saw Eva, he just hasn't dared, and now that he does dare . . .

It was sometime last winter, he knows that, because there had been a light fall of snow on the sierra and the cold was intense. He'd heard a scrabbling at his door so faint he wasn't sure he'd heard anything at first; then, thinking it might be a stray animal, he'd gone to take a look.

He'd found Eva standing there, her face filled to overflowing with barely suppressed emotion and a bottle of Tonayán in her hand.

—I hate him—she'd said.

Arturo didn't need to ask who. They stood in the doorway for a moment before Eva spoke again.

—Arturo. I'm cold.

—Sorry. It's not much warmer in here—he said.

But he invited her in and he tried to coax a little more heat out of his makeshift stove. He threw on some really good scrap wood he'd been saving for the worst of the cold, and found a mug to use as a glass. He handed it to Eva, and she laughed and pulled the cork from the bottle, drinking from it directly.

She handed the bottle to Arturo.

—Here—she said, and he drank, while Eva told him about the fight she'd had with Faustino.

Arturo couldn't really follow what Eva was saying, and now, all this time later, Arturo cannot even really remember the little he did understand. But it seemed that Faustino had been with another girl. Or maybe just kissed her. Or, and Arturo wasn't even sure about this, maybe he had only said he would *like* to kiss her, and then there'd been a big fight. Arturo didn't follow the details because he wasn't really interested. All he could think was that if two people were lucky enough to have someone to be with, then why should they ever fight about anything? Couldn't they just be happy that they had someone? Wasn't that enough?

But Eva was getting drunker and Arturo was catching up fast, drinking bad mezcal and, since there hadn't been much to eat recently, drinking it on an empty stomach. Soon, none of the things Eva was talking about seemed to matter, not to Arturo, not to Eva herself.

They began to laugh and joke and Eva dried her tears. They talked about old days, days when they were kids, days when the boys were still going to school. Arturo mentioned the thing with the handprints and the paint.

—I never thought you liked me again, after that—he said.

Eva looked surprised.

—¿No? ¿Really?

—Not in the same way. I think you never forgot it.

Eva laughed, but it was a strange sort of laugh.

—No, Arturo. No, I liked you just as much.

—It didn't seem that way—said Arturo, shrugging, taking another swig of Tonayán.

As he lowered the bottle, he found Eva looking at him very seriously, leaning in close.

—No, Arturo—she said.—I liked you just as much.

As Arturo lies on his bed, thinking about that night, thinking about how drunk they got, he cannot remember any more details of what they said. He doesn't remember, for example, what he said next, but he supposes he must have said something because somehow Eva was moving closer to him. They looked right into each other, even through the mezcal, and then Arturo remembers slipping Eva's jacket off, and then she pulled her T-shirt off over her head and it was cold in the shack, despite the fire in the stove. But Arturo remembers how their skin was warm, he remembers how wonderful it felt to feel their soft bare skin pressing against each other as they slid down under his blanket. He remembers sliding the rest of Eva's clothes from her body, and there was something funny about that, though what it was has long since left him. It's not important. And anyway, most of all he remembers that, even in the very moment, he guessed there could be no better feeling in the world than that: folding around and around and into someone else; safe, warm, naked.

He never saw Eva again. She left before he had even woken to a charging hangover. For the whole of the first day he expected to see her coming along the street, to be with him, to talk. She didn't, yet in the coming days, as he realized she had just made a mistake, that she didn't want to be with him instead of Faustino, he still expected her to show up. To come and talk things over, to explain, to say sorry, maybe. At the very least, to tell him never to whisper a word of what had happened to Faustino, should they ever run into each other. But she never came, and neither did Faustino, not until they both showed up last night, with a car, and a baby.

A one-month-old baby.

Arturo knows he cannot be sure. He will never be sure. There is no way of telling. But he does know that it was just after Christmas when she came; that it's just about ten months since that night when Eva showed up, angry and drunk, and they got lost in each other, and when, for a very short time, Arturo was saved.

More Mexicans are leaving the US than migrating there, a study by the Pew Research Center has found.

More than one million Mexicans and their families, including US-born children, returned to Mexico during the period 2009–2014.

Meanwhile, around 870,000 Mexicans moved to the US over the same period, creating a net loss of 140,000 people.

Hardliners claim that these figures do not reflect the true picture since they can only estimate the flow of illegal aliens, while others say the figures show that increased border controls have made it harder for undocumented Mexicans to enter the United States, that fences can work. There is another argument, unspoken by almost everyone, which reasons that perhaps Mexicans are simply returning home—and for a good reason: because they want to.

VISITORS

Five o'clock comes and goes. There is no sign of Faustino.

Damn you, damn you, damn you, thinks Arturo. Damn you, cabrón. My friend. My brother. Damn you.

He waits on the box he uses as a bench outside his door, until he gets too cold and begins to pace up and down the street to keep warm. The sound of every engine has him craning his neck and straining his eyes, but no cars come up Isla de Sacrificios; he sees just a few passing in the distance, and none of them is Faustino's white Ford.

He gives up, tells himself he won't come if he stands outside waiting like an anxious mother. There is that, and the fact that the sun is setting. Arturo does not want to see the sun set, and as the sky begins to burn orange at first, and then redder and redder, he slinks back into his shack. He sees his pack of calavera cards sitting on the table. He picks them up, silently denouncing them. He goes to the stove and tries to light the remains of the last fire he had. He just about gets it to catch, and as soon as it's burning, he begins to flick the cards into the flames, one by one, waiting until each one has caught, then flicking another in, precisely, adding to the fire.

He stares at the flames, remembering his dream of the night before; his dream of fire and water. He hadn't thought of it before, but someone once told him what it means to dream of water. He tries to remember who it was. He is about to flick another card into the flames when he realizes he has one in his hand already. It's a five.

He stares at it, and the skin creeps on the back of his neck. He stares at the five little red hearts; the square of four outside, and one all alone, in the middle. As he stares at the heart in the middle, he hears an engine outside.

He turns toward the door, and, still holding the five, he remembers who it was who told him what it means to dream of water, for she is right there, getting out of a gold Jeep, the only one who ever really taught him anything: Margarita.

She's by herself.

She looks worried. Scared even.

She hurries over to Arturo, throws her arms around him.

—¡Niño!—she says.—¡You poor kid! ¡I'm sorry!

Arturo steps away. He wonders what it is that she's sorry for, and is about to tell her she has nothing to be sorry for, but she won't stop talking.

—I had no idea. He told me you were dead. ¿Why would I not believe him? He would never say more; refused to talk about it. But I told him, Arturo. I told him, after you left; I said that he had to tell me everything else, and that if I ever found another lie coming from his lips, I will leave. I will take your sister and leave.

Arturo shakes his head.

—¿So you know? ¿You know he works for the Azteca?

Margarita is silenced, briefly.

—Of course I know—she says quietly.—But do not think badly of me, Arturo. All he does is drive.

All he does is drive, Arturo thinks. He knows that Margarita knows that the driving he does is not so innocent. He thinks about Gabriel, being bundled into Raúl's pickup. He thinks about the bodies that dangle from the overpasses, messages of terror carved into their skin. He thinks about the charred remains of those executed by necklacing. He wonders if his father has driven those bodies, those people, to their ultimate destinations.

—Don't judge me—says Margarita.—¿You think I had it easy, as a teacher, here? Sure, I had a better job than some. I didn't have to go to a maquiladora every day. But there aren't so many choices for a woman here. I wasn't making much as a teacher and that was before the M-33 came to the school. They told every teacher that half our salary would go to them from then on . . . So when I saw my chance, I got out. I wanted a better life, Arturo. I wanted a better life. ¿Is that so bad?

Arturo finds it hard to argue with what Margarita is saying. And yet she is now well off, rich even, because his father has thrown himself in with *the life*, as they say. And the way they make their money is through drugs, through killing people who get in their way, through the wielding of absurd amounts of power. Power that can defy anything, defeat anyone, corrupt anyone; even the police, even politicians. It's a drug that is too powerful to resist; once tasted, it takes hold of people, sometimes even good people. And the question of who is clean, and who is sucio, dirty, is not so simple in Juárez. It's not so black and white. And while you might not be *in the life*, there are matters like who spends money in your shop, or bar, or who paid to build the church you worship in. There's the matter of who paid you not to write something in the newspaper, there's the business of what your son is doing every night that you try so hard to ignore.

There's an equation that says if you're clean, then the gangs won't want anything to do with you. You'll be safe. It's an equation that goes on to say that if you happen to get raped or killed, then it must be because the gangs did want something from you, and therefore you *were* dirty, all along. There's no escaping that logic, but it's blind logic that helps people pretend that the world isn't going mad all around them. The truth is much harder to find, and Margarita is proof of that.

Now that he sees her again, away from his father, Arturo can see the other dark thing in her eyes, which he could not see before. Yes, that's it. There is *shame*. And Arturo finds he cannot blame her for her choice, despite everything it means, because he can still hear Carlos's words in his head. *Everything, Arturo. They're scared of everything.*

But really, none of this matters now.

—¿Why have you come?—Arturo asks, and, hurriedly, Margarita starts rummaging in her bag.

—I told him, I said. I told him. You have to give Arturo the money he needs. He's your son. That is something you cannot deny. Something you must be true to. And I told him if he wants me to stay around and stick with him, the first thing he had to do was give you the money you need. So I found out where you live from Carlos and Siggy and here it is.

She's smiling, she's holding out an envelope, bulging from whatever's inside. Money. Margarita has brought him money, from his father.

It's Santa Muerte.

Arturo knows that she has saved him, after all. She has been playing with him, testing his faith, teasing him, for what he did at Doña Maria's, but finally, she has performed a miracle. Or maybe, Arturo thinks, it's Margarita who's performed the miracle, because she has talked his father, his useless, unloving, wreck of a father, into giving him the five thousand dollars.

He tears the envelope open, with good tears in his eyes, and then he freezes.

—¿What's this?—he asks.

He has taken the money out and is holding it for Margarita to see.

—It's the money you need, of course—she's saying, but the smile is faltering on her face.—The money you need. Roberto told me you need five hundred dollars.

Arturo cannot speak. He's holding five hundred dollars in one hand, and an empty envelope in the other. No, it's not quite empty. He sees there is a slip of paper inside. It has writing on it. He twists his hand so he can see the note without taking it out of the envelope, without touching it.

He reads.

You are a tenth of the son you should be.
Here is a tenth of the money you need.

211

Somewhere above Arturo, somewhere out of sight, Santa Muerte is watching him, watching to see what he does next. The world starts folding in on itself again, a loud vibrating stagger, a staccato shudder, focused around a point in space that seems to lie directly between Arturo's hands. It threatens to rip and pour into itself, sucking him and everything else with it.

Margarita is speaking to him; he doesn't hear her. He cannot hear over the sound of the universe shaking itself to bits inside him.

—¿Margarita?—Arturo says, though he can only just hear himself above the noise.

—¿Yes?

—You once told me what it means to dream of water. ¿Didn't you?

Margarita is shaking her head.

—Yes, I did . . . But—

—¿What does it mean? To dream of water.

—Nothing, Arturo. It means nothing. I cannot—

—It's okay—says Arturo.

He knows anyway, he has remembered what it means. It's okay. The meaning is coming, very soon. There is no need to question, no need to worry. There is no more danger.

—¿Margarita?—he says, finally looking up from the money in his hands.

—¿What is it, Arturo? ¿Do you need more money? He has the money, your father, and I don't—

—I want you to do something for me—Arturo says.—Right now.

Margarita is nodding, though her face is filled with confusion.

212

—Yes, of course. ¿What can I do?

Arturo knows what he has to do, he knows what Santa Muerte wants him to do. The new thought that entered his head as a tiny seed has planted itself and grown and is already bursting through his mind, a wild forest of leaves. And it's okay, it's okay, it's really okay, only something is distracting him, something on the edge of his vision and at the corner of his hearing. He shakes his head, as if trying to shoo blowflies away. There must be no distractions. Not now. He needs just a moment of clarity, a moment of calm, in which to test the beliefs of his friends, the barroom philosophers. He will try to prove Carlos right, and Siggy wrong.

—I want you to take this money. ¿Do you know Chaveña? There's a street called Libertad. Number 965. Go there now before it gets dark, it's not a safe place. Go there and give this money to Faustino.

The distraction is buzzing louder, getting closer, and Arturo gets worried now, because Margarita is shaking her head.

—No—she says.—No, I can't. No, you have to take it. Arturo, listen to me. Whatever trouble—

—Take it, Margarita—says Arturo.—Take it to Faustino. Faustino needs it. ¿You understand?

He's speaking more firmly now, more insistently. She has to take it, she has to take the money to Faustino and she has to take it now, because Arturo cannot ignore the distraction anymore: as he looks down the length of Isla de Sacrificios, he sees a dark-red pickup swing into view. He knew it was coming, somehow, before he saw it, and now here it is, conjured into his vision.

¿Did I conjure it? he thinks. ¿Or did she? ¿The Bony Lady?

It's not traveling fast, but it will be here in a matter of seconds. Nevertheless, Arturo has all the time he needs. He knows that he is on the bridge. Siggy told him that, Carlos too. He also knows that he has been on the bridge for a long time, and that, even though the truck is moments away, there is still plenty of time to get to the end.

Arturo stares at Margarita. Then he pulls the five hundred dollars that Carlos gave him from his pocket and shoves it in the envelope with his father's money.

—Margarita, for your baby's sake, get out of here. Take this and leave now. ¡Now!

She sees what he is looking at, the red truck, and her whole face trembles because she understands what is coming down the road toward them. Without another word, she takes the money and slides into the seat of her car and starts the engine.

Arturo backs away, trying not to make it look like anything, that nothing is going on between them. Just a conversation between strangers, and nothing more, but as she's about to pull away, Arturo says one more thing through her open window.

—Tell Faustino tomorrow has come. Give him the money and tell him tomorrow has come.

She goes.

The pickup is twenty meters away.

Arturo watches it come, calmly. He can see Raúl behind the wheel, he can see a couple of other guys in the back. As it rolls toward him he has all the time he needs to understand everything.

Thoughts that might take a lifetime to discover, never mind to understand, are revealed to him in simple, bright colors and shapes.

There is no escaping the truck that is coming for him; there is no escaping the end, not for him. But Faustino . . . Faustino can do a lot with a thousand dollars. He can give El Carnero all his money back. He can return the money he stole, and go on being a falcon for Los Libertadores. Very soon they'll make him one of the gang; he can get money, be rich, he can even become a sicario, a hitman, and make money by killing people with that American gun of his. He could do all of that. Or he could do something else, something better.

He could leave.

He could pay the same coyotes who took Eva and leave, tonight. He could pay the coyotes five hundred to get to LA and take Eva away from there. With the five hundred left over he can find a place to stay while they get themselves sorted. Head north, away from the pandillas, the drugs, the killings. There might even be somewhere in the world that is safe.

Arturo thinks about his brother, Faustino, and knows he'll understand the message. Tomorrow has come. Faustino will know what to do. Take this chance, a chance somehow made by Santa Muerte, of that, Arturo is sure. Take this chance to run, and yes, he will need to be careful, but Faustino is not stupid. He can do it, take care of himself and make things right for him, and for Eva, and the baby.

The baby, which might be Faustino's, or which might not. Arturo knows it doesn't matter. Because if there's just the slightest chance that the baby is *his*, then he can be a better father to the baby like this than his own father ever was to *him*. He will never see his son again, he never even really looked at him, but if Faustino can find Eva and the baby, and make things work, that won't matter. It will be good.

The truck is ten meters away, then five, crawling to a stop.

Arturo realizes that the world stopped shaking and he didn't even notice, that the evening air is tranquil and still, that nothing moves save Raúl's pickup, and now even that comes to rest right beside him.

Raúl leans out of the open window. A gun lolls easily in his hand.

—¿You got the money?—he asks.

Arturo shakes his head.

—I was hoping you'd say that—Raúl says through his face of tattooed power. He pops the door open suddenly, but then stops, surprised. There is no need to threaten Arturo, no need for the narcos in the back, because Arturo is climbing up into the cab.

—I guess El Carnero wants to see me. ¿Right?

Raúl laughs. Arturo is not sure why, but it doesn't matter. The truck pulls away from Isla de Sacrificios and Arturo doesn't look back.

Above him, in the dusk on the hilltop, Christ the King stands with his arms outstretched.

UNBEHAGEN

Arturo leaves with the second of his three visitors, driven away in a red pickup by a man with a tattooed face and an automatic pistol sitting on the dash by his left hand.

The third of his visitors is late, he is far too late.

Faustino tried to drive west, to Janos, where he hoped to borrow the money from a distant relative of Eva's mother who runs a flower shop there. It was a long shot anyway, one he never got to try. His piece of crap car died in the desert not even halfway there and he's spent the day walking back to Juárez, a journey that could have killed him if he'd tried it in the heat of the summer. He tried to thumb a lift from the few cars and trucks that went by, but no one stopped, leaving him to hobble on, toward the city, coming in from the west, a way that takes him right up Rancho Anapra.

It's there that Margarita passes him. She hasn't seen him in years, but she knows it's him, the limp making him unmistakable even from a distance.

She pulls to a stop beside him, waving at him frantically, telling him to get in. Faustino is too tired to be surprised, but when Margarita hands him an envelope with a thousand dollars, he knows that Santa Muerte has protected him once more. As Margarita hurriedly tries to explain what has happened, Faustino crosses himself, and thanks the Skinny Girl for looking out for him. As if further proof were needed, Faustino sees where Margarita and he have met: right outside Doña Maria's house.

Faustino starts to ask her to take him to Chaveña; there is still time to get back to Libertad and restore this thousand dollars to its brethren, before El Carnero comes tonight, but then, Margarita is telling him something else.

—¡Faustino!—she says.—¡Listen to me! Arturo is in some kind of trouble. He needs money.

—Yes, I know—Faustino says.—He needed a thousand dollars to save my stupid skin. But we've got it now. I've got it. It's all okay.

Then Margarita explains why it is not okay. She tells Faustino what she knows about the mess Arturo is in. She tells him about the message. She tells him about the red pickup truck that just rolled down Isla de Sacrificios.

—¿What?—he asks.—¿You're sure? ¿A red Toyota?

And when Margarita nods, Faustino feels things sliding out of his grasp, rapidly.

—We have to go there—he says.—We have to go back.

Margarita shakes her head.

—Faustino, I'm scared.

—¡We have to go back! ¡Now!

Still Margarita hesitates.

—Faustino, I have a baby at home. She needs me. She—

Faustino waves his hand at Doña Maria's house.

—You can stay here, if you like. Just let me have the car. Or I'll walk.

He starts to get out of the car, and Margarita puts her hand on his shoulder.

—¡No! Okay, we'll go. Get back in. We'll go.

They drive the short way to Isla de Sacrificios, fearing what they will see, dreading that Arturo will be gone, terrified that the red pickup will still be there.

It isn't. It's gone, and so is Arturo.

They get out of the Jeep to be sure, and check inside the shack.

Nothing. Half a pack of calavera cards lying on the floor, a slight smell of burning plastic from the stove. The bed.

They stumble back out into the twilight of Anapra. Margarita stares at the dirt at her feet, Faustino cannot draw his eyes away from the tiny shack where his brother has been living in the time they have been apart.

—They've taken him—Margarita says eventually.

—Then he's already dead.

They stay that way for a long time, not speaking, as the night comes on and the darkness deepens. A stray dog wanders past, sniffing for the boy who lives in the jacal. The air cools.

Finally, Faustino stirs. There is no easy way to pretend to himself that he is doing the right thing, the sensible thing. But in the face of Arturo's death, that seems less important, and the only thing that matters now is tomorrow.

—Margarita, there's a cattle market just down the road west. Right on the border. ¿Do you know it? ¿Could you take me there?

She nods.

—¿What are you going to do?

Faustino opens the door to the Jeep, and as he's getting in, he's thinking about his friend.

—I'm going to do what Arturo wanted me to.

BEWEGUNG

Arturo is not dead, but he is dying.

They have hurt him very badly. They have not finished with him yet.

That is yet to come, and there is still time to look away.

To begin with, El Carnero smiled, in just the same way he had over the calavera table from time to time. Raúl had pulled Arturo from the truck, through the tumult of El Alacrán, and then into a room behind the bar, where it seemed El Carnero had his own private shrine to Santa Muerte.

As Arturo was brought in, El Carnero turned away from some devotion he was making to the White Sister. There she was, once more, and Arturo could see that she was still staring at him, still never once blinking. El Carnero's shrine was somehow different than Doña Maria's. Here, there were two tables; a long one right up against the wall, covered in a black cloth. Upon that table stood glasses of water, tequila, and beer. Plastic roses, carnations, and cempasúchil placed in empty beer bottles. Trays of money, little round dishes with packets of weed and wraps of coke nestling in them. There were three small figures of the girl herself, each with a different color of robe: one gold, one black, one red. Otherwise, the figures were all the same: the scythe in one hand, the world in the other.

In front of the long table was a lower, circular one, again covered in cloth, this time red, and it was on this table that the main figure of Santa Muerte stood. She was finely made, from plaster, her dress of green, and, again, the scythe and the world held out.

Around her, on the floor, on the wall behind the tables, in fact everywhere, were other figures, bewildering. Arturo saw them all. He knew what some were: prints of Jesús Malverde, paper cuts of La Catrina. Then there were figurines of Apache and Sioux warriors, a row of little wooden owls. A statue of Buddha. Dozens of candles, in a rainbow of colors.

El Carnero stood, the bottle of Rancho Viejo still in his hand, and Arturo saw what he had been doing: topping up a glass of tequila placed at the Skinny Girl's feet.

—She likes to get drunk sometimes—El Carnero said.—Just like the rest of us. ¿Right?

Arturo said nothing. He wondered whether she had helped him at all. He wondered whether he would have been better ignoring Faustino's pleas for help, his insistence that Santa Muerte would save them.

Then El Carnero set the bottle down and came over to Arturo.

—You know, I never expected you to find the money.

Arturo nodded, still saying nothing, and all he could think was, Let it be quick, let it be quick, let it be quick.

El Carnero pulled a couple of chairs into the center of the room. He sat, and pointed at the other chair.

Arturo looked at the chair. He stayed standing.

El Carnero raised his eyebrows for a moment, then shrugged.

—So you might want to ask me what this is all about—El Carnero suggested.

Arturo still said nothing.

El Carnero sighed, but the smile was long gone from his face now.

—I am offering you a choice—he said.—I will wipe your debt to me, wipe it clean. And all you have to do is something for me, Eduardo Cardona. El Carnero.

Arturo's head tilted fractionally. His eyes narrowed.

—¿What?

—I want you to work for me. I always need more guys, so that's what I'm offering, but as I said, I am offering you a choice. So the first option is, you can work for me. I can tell you're a smart kid.

He didn't say what the other option was. There was no need. Raúl stood in the corner of the room, and Arturo could hear him breathing, could feel his heat. Arturo knew he had reached the other side of the bridge, and Siggy was right, it had been a dangerous time. It had been a long and dangerous journey, but Arturo had made it. There was no danger anymore. He looked ahead. He saw the life that was being offered to him; he saw the money. He saw the power. He saw the cars. He saw the drugs, he saw the fighting. He saw the torture and the executions. He saw women to be used as objects. He saw his father, and the life he had chosen. He saw it all, and then, from nowhere, it was replaced by something else, something worth much more than all the money and power in the world. Finally, he understood what he had been looking for; he understood what everyone has been looking for since they were pulled away from the universe, away from one-ness, and left to manage on their own, as individuals adrift in civilization. He realized how we squatted around campfires in dark caves, he knew how we were alone, everywhere alone. He knew how we made promises around those campfires, promises in which we agreed to be as one, in order that we should *not* be alone. How we made prints of our hands on the walls of the caves, prints to seal the promises. ¿But will we keep those promises? thought Arturo. That's the question. ¿Can we?

Arturo stood, still as the world, and there is time, still, to look away.

He faced El Carnero, and El Carnero smiled his smile, thinking that Arturo was going to say *yes. Yes, I will work for you.*

—No—said Arturo, and he knew there was no danger anymore because now everything would happen just as he knew it would. He could be the man that El Carnero wanted him to be, but he knew he had not crossed the bridge to become that man; a man who would only add more horror to the world, more pain. Instead, he chose the path that had been revealed to him only this morning, as he stumbled from El Diván, and he knew there was no danger anymore.

El Carnero stared at him, silent. Raúl had stopped breathing, for the moment, and into that silence, Arturo said his last words.

—I want to belong to something. But not that. Not that.

They beat him. First El Carnero, laughing as he threw his punches, while Raúl held Arturo tight, but he soon got bored, and hobbled back into the heaving night of the bar. Then Arturo was left alone with Raúl, who beat him with a crowbar, and kicked him when he collapsed to the ground. There was no need even to tape his hands. Then Raúl found a hammer, and a knife, the kind of knife used for slicing open packs of meat, and he set to work.

When he was done, he wrapped Arturo in a sheet and threw him in the back of the pickup. He drove out into the city to the border and there he dumped the body on the bank of the river. He was about to drive away when he saw that Arturo was still moving.

He is not yet dead, but very soon it will be too late to look away.

Though there is nothing to fear, there is pain; unimaginable pain. Arturo's body screams as it perishes, though his own screams stopped long ago; there is no energy left for that; he feels almost nothing. He is covered in his own blood, his body is broken and destroyed, he cannot see, though Raúl has not yet managed to destroy his mind. The final thing to arrive in Arturo's mind is an image, a picture from long ago, of three handprints on the school wall. He remembers he chose red paint to cover his hand. As he lies on the ground, his arm twisted out in front of him, it seems to Arturo that the red paint has returned. He remembers promises made.

Raúl stands behind Arturo, looking down at the shape in the

sheet by the bank of the river, wondering if it was some trick of the light that made him think he saw movement. He takes a half step back as the shape moves again, and then, somehow, Arturo manages to pull the sheet off him, and roll to one side.

Raúl raises the gun, pointing at the back of Arturo's head.

Forcing his bloody hand against the ground, pushing himself up on a shattered arm, Arturo manages to get to his knees, wavering, unsteady, heedless of the terrible bursts of pain that return with every movement.

Behind Arturo is Juárez; the laboratory. Juárez, the ultimate goal, our final destination; the logical conclusion to the world we are making, and look away if you want; it's there nonetheless.

In front of Arturo is the river, the fences, and El Norte, all waiting to watch the end. Arturo sways on his knees, his hearing fading and failing, and then he opens his arms; somehow his arms are outstretched, but they are not outstretched because they are nailed to a cross.

There is a terrible sudden roar and the shaking world breaks in two. Through the cleft pour the writhing gods of old, who circle Arturo, wanting the blood they have come to witness, and Arturo does not disappoint them. He has become one of the dirty saints now, an unwashed martyr, a grubby sacrifice, and it is time, la hora de la hora. Only yesterday did he wonder whether he wanted to destroy something, or create something, and now he knows for sure that it is both; he just had no idea that the thing he would be destroying and creating would be himself. Yet just as predicted, he dies the death he was looking for. He dies, his body in motion one last time, and he dies for many reasons, for many people.

He dies for Santa Muerte, although, at this, the culmination, she is not here to watch. It's all the same to her; they all come in the end, they all do.

He dies for his friends, Carlos and Siggy, and now he understands the thing that El Alemán once said: when you cross a bridge, there is always a price to pay.

He dies for Faustino. He sees his friend out there in the desert, tonight, running toward a new life in America.

He dies for Eva. He sees one last flash of that night, the night she came, and he remembers what was so funny when he undressed her: Mickey Mouse on her underwear, and he thought, ¡My God, we're just children! ¿When do we stop being children?

He dies for Ana, Gabriel's wife, knowing we cannot walk away from people's screams forever.

He dies for Anapra, and for Juárez.

He dies for Mexico, for America.

He dies for his half-sister and his son. He dies for everyone. He dies for the world.

But does he die for these things?

Is it a noble death, a meaningful sacrifice, one to make us recall our dark-cave promises? Will statues be erected in his honor, will the gods themselves bow down and say, There goes Arturo; Arturo the King?

Or does he die for nothing?

This book is inspired by the writings of:
Charles Bowden, Noam Chomsky, John Dodson,
Sigmund Freud, Cynthia Gorney, Anne Huffschmid,
Carl Jung, Claudio Lomnitz, Karl Marx, Sonia Nazario,
Octavio Paz, and Arthur Schnitzler.

I would like to thank Gaby Silva-Rivero and
Sergio Camacho for their invaluable help.